BLEAK

HOUSES

Published by Raw Dog Screaming Press

Bowie, MD

First Edition

Cover art copyright 2023 by Lynne Hansen

LynneHansenArt.com

Printed in the United States of America

This is a work of fiction. Any resemblance to persons living or dead is unintentional.

ISBN: 978-1-947879-59-1

Library of Congress Control Number: 2023935796

RawDogScreaming.com

BLEAK HOUSES

Safer

&

Family Solstice

Kate Maruyama

For Kit and Joe, game changers

Selected Papers

 from the Consortium for the Study of

Anomalous Phenomena

Mom didn't want me to take the job at first. I wonder now if she knew, somehow.

She said, "You'll be living in their house, mija. How much of a creep is the dad?" She had gotten a little too into the whole Schwarzenegger housekeeper scandal and worried for any domestic worker friend out there. *People* magazine was her drug of choice.

"Mom, I can take care of myself. Damn." Plus, what else was I going to do with the summer of COVID? Los Angeles was in full lockdown. The restaurant where I used to work lucrative weekend shifts was closed. I had two more years of college and the online jobs were all taken. It's not like the preschool where I worked was reopening any time soon. And there was no seeing anybody during this thing. If I got this job, at least I'd be around people again. I seriously missed people. Going from two jobs and packed classes to my own four walls was too much too fast. I needed this.

"Where is it?" She was frying something sizzly. I missed her meals like crazy and hanging with her when she cooked. But two years this side of breast cancer, she was at risk, and we were keeping each other safe. Sure, she left me Tupperware full of food when I dropped off groceries, but it wasn't the same.

"Up in Beachwood Canyon or something. It's called Wolf's Lair?"

She gasped. "Moby owned that place for years. It's supposed to be haunted!" *People* magazine strikes again.

"Haunted how?" I heard that edge coming into my voice I sometimes got with my mom, and it made me feel bad, since I saw her so seldom these days, but I knew I was in for some line of haunted celebrity bullshit she'd picked up from *E! Online* or something.

"He sold it to 'Anonymous.' You're going to work for Anonymous! Oh my God, take some pictures, will you? Maybe leave your camera on when you walk around? You *have* to tell me who Anonymous is."

"It's an interview, Ma. I don't think filming it would look good."

"Then you'd better get that job."

All her cautionary tales had somehow fallen away for a chance that her kid might work for someone famous enough to gossip about.

That Friday I used Mom's Camry to curbside pickup their week's groceries at Ralphs which I dropped off on their front stoop in Temple City. I went back to her car before I texted her. She was always threatening to hug me, which scared the crap out of me. I was not going to be the one to kill my parents.

Of course she was at the door in a minute flat, pulling on her flowered mask she'd made from an old tablecloth, toting a bag chock full of Tupperwares of food. Mami hadn't ever quite learned how to cook for fewer than eight people, so there were always leftovers. She FaceTimed me the night before while she was cooking, so I knew it was birria, Guadalajara style, of course. Dad was from Oaxaca but Mami's cuisine ruled the house.

Her hair had gone gray because of the lack of a hairdresser, and I could swear she was shorter. COVID was sucking the life force out of my parents, out of all of us.

"Come in for a minute. We'll just keep our masks on." She started walking toward me.

I stepped around the driver side of the car to put the car between us. "Ma, don't start. Plus, I have that interview."

She squealed with excitement like a pre-teen girl. "Anonymous! It's someone really famous, I just know it is. Text me when you're there."

I opened the car door and the threat of my getting into the car slowed her progress as she got too close to me. "I gotta go, I'm late. I love you. Don't forget to wash all the groceries. I'll bring the car back when I'm done." Mom and Dad were over an hour bus ride from my apartment, but this was how we roll.

She shook her head and waved me away. "Wash the groceries. It's stupid."

Jesus Christ, my parents were going to die, and it was going to be because my mom didn't listen. I said, "Wash the groceries for me, Ma, I mean it. Do I have to send you another article?"

"No, no. Enough with your articles. This is nuts."

"You're nuts. I love you. I gotta go."

She waved and then labored under a bag of groceries, and I realized I should have split up the carrots and potatoes into separate bags. I wondered when my larger than life, fierce, hilarious Mami had gotten so old. I backed out of the driveway before she thought of anything else to say.

I got off on Vine Street in Hollywood and headed up Beachwood Canyon, past sweet 1930s apartment houses whose rent cost more than a mortgage in the San Gabriel Valley. Within three blocks up Beachwood, the noise of the city was behind me and the quiet of residential neighborhood took over. I rolled down my windows to let in the June afternoon air. The warming sun, faint exhaust, and something wonderful blooming flooded the car.

The Hollywood sign shone clear and full across the Mount Lee that hovered in front of me at the end of the road. I knew better than to try to photograph it from here, the naked eye makes everything seem closer than it really is. But it didn't prevent tourists in the rental Sonata ahead of me from screeching to a stop and stepping in the middle of the road to take a picture. I swerved to avoid them. What a thing to be a tourist in this locked down city. I wondered if the lack of traffic made up for the fact that everything was closed: Universal Studios, all the Hollywood tours. Screeching to a halt on Beachwood was likely all they had.

I drove through the Hollywoodland stone gate, the early 20th century brainchild of the same realty company that had erected the Hollywood sign. An earthquake had taken the "land" down decades before.

I banged a sharp left after the Beachwood Café. I'd been up in this canyon once or twice to a party in a floating trailer, which is what I called those 1970s cliff dwellings that hung off the edge of the Hollywood hills, held up by I-beams plunged into the hill beneath them. Dotted in among the trailers were really pretty 1930s houses of varying kinds. Some had minor entryways off the winding roads to houses that dropped down the hill three stories behind. Because a lot of set designers settled here in the thirties, they were built in all styles. Classic Spanish houses gave way to witchy little cottages and one, I swear that looked like it could only be inhabited by Hobbits. Others topped with Moorish whipped cream dollop turrets and covered in leaded stained-glass windows looked like the kind of place where silent film stars would live, draped over fur rugs on their terra cotta floors, living a life of debauchery. At least that's what I liked to imagine. I wondered what it would be like to be so debt free you could live up here and had time for debauchery.

The road to Wolf's Lair was so narrow and winding I had to pull over twice for Amazon trucks. I wound around Belden, took a sharp turn to the left that took me in the opposite direction up, up, further up. Houses gave way to a curved gray stone wall that rose up to the right of the car, looming beyond what I could see. I passed a sinister looking black metal gate behind which a steep set of stairs climbed up into the wall. As I'd been asked to, I pulled into the drive and stopped at a gate that hinted at medieval portcullis. The metal gate was lined with white painted wood so you couldn't see through it. I imagined my mom squealing with excitement at what it hid. Its archway matched a gothic doorway to its right. The gate led through a turreted building topped with a white tower, like a mini version of the castle itself. It was referred to as a castle anywhere its name came up, but I hadn't prepared myself for its gray stone walls, princess towers, and impregnability.

I texted the mom, Celine, that I had arrived. After a long moment, right before I felt like I had waited too long and almost texted again, the gate swung open. Was Celine Anonymous? Maybe she was married to Anonymous.

I drove through a passageway under the building, also lined in gray stone and the driveway sloped above me. I gunned the car a little to get to the … driveway? Parking lot? I couldn't think what to call the massive, paved space in front of the house with a carport that housed a very nice state of the art Tesla station wagon. At least they cared about the planet...rich family style.

Celine stood on the front porch. She was blonde, slim, tanned, but healthy, and looked expensive. She was already wearing a mask, so I pulled on my N95 and called up the photo of my negative COVID test results on my phone before I got out of the car, per the directions in her lengthy email. I held out the phone at arm's length and from about ten feet away, she leaned in tentatively, and squinted. She wouldn't step any closer.

She shrugged and said, "I'm sorry, I don't think I can...see it." There was this helpless tone rich people got, I encountered it a lot at my table waiting job. It meant, do more, because they weren't going to help.

I said, "Maybe if we go somewhere in the shade?" Was she checking if it was fake or something? Seriously?

She stuttered, "It's negative, right?"

I tried not to laugh. I put on my most comforting dealing with difficult parents smile. "It's negative...or I wouldn't have come."

"Well, I'm glad you're being responsible." There was something doubtful to her tone, cautionary and doubtful? White ladies were always laying code into what they said, and I could never fully make it out. It definitely felt like a judgment. I smized my hardest from behind my N95 and nodded as she led me around the back of the house. The place was amazing, turreted like a castle, painted white with gray stonework and gothic arched windows. Next to those 1970s floating trailers hovering out over the canyon, littered with bamboo roll-up shades against the sun and too many wind chimes, it was completely otherworldly.

This would not be a bad place to spend quarantine. Sure as shit beat my one bedroom studio I'd just moved into in Glendale near the college. I didn't mind the smallness of the space when I chose it, I figured I'd be on campus all day and I was saving a bundle in rent. I didn't count on 2020.

But no one had.

If we stayed quarantined in the fall maybe I could extend my stay a little. Take classes online from one of these turreted rooms.

I had some friends who seemed to be living in an alternate universe outside the pandemic. Went about like things were still normal, complained about their restaurants closing, whined about school being remote. But I had a lot of old people in my family I wasn't about to kill. My abuelitos, my parents. No way. I locked down like they told me when they told me and honestly, friends who didn't, I kinda let go. You either gave a shit or you didn't.

The back of the house had a kidney bean shaped pool, not outrageously big, but its deck was expensively lined with squares of stone in natural hues from red to beige. Celine motioned to some swanky cushioned lawn furniture on the back patio under an overhang, which was arranged next to a fireplace.

I don't know how these people got their money, but they had plenty, that's for sure.

Celine walked a good ten feet away from me and sank onto a chaise lounge followed by her flowing linen skirt-overalls type thing that looked like it was designed and sewn together by a five-year-old, but likely cost hundreds of dollars. She was the epitome of the LA's 1980s idea of beauty. Too skinny, skin tanned, but nourished somehow. Like some crazy all organic vegan nonsense diet had made her the picture of health on a cellular level.

I sat on the sofa opposite her, suddenly self-conscious about my own body, which was called thick on good days, fat on bad days. At least my brown was real all the time, and didn't need spraying on or sun damage to keep up. I reminded myself I was here for a job and movie people were the reason there were eating disorders.

She motioned to a glass on the table in front of me. "Disinfected, I promise,"

It was weird taking my mask off in front of anyone. Since lockdown had started, I hadn't removed it anywhere but in my apartment. I motioned to my mask. Celine nodded, "Absolutely. You're far enough away, I'm leaving mine on."

This world. How strange everything felt after isolation. Like we didn't know how to be. And Celine's steady blue gaze added to that feeling. Part of me wanted to beg off, not thirsty, but since she'd served me, I was obligated. I knew every move I made was being sized up. From removing the mask to accepting the water.

She said, "Of course, if you come to work with us, you'll just be living here, and we all can relax a little." She laughed in that self-conscious loud way reserved for popular girls at parties.

"So, when can I meet…I'm sorry, you never told me his name."

"Story."

"Story." I never understood Hollywood names. Apple. X AE. Blanket, whatever. It'd be nice to hang out with a kid again, though. It had been three months since I'd even seen one, when I used to spend my days surrounded at the daycare.

Celine said, "I have a few questions first. Do you speak Spanish?"

"Yes, I speak a little with family, but not enough to teach, I don't think."

She had this way of staring at me when I talked. It wasn't overtly judgmental, but it definitely wasn't passive. She weighed everything I said. It felt like I was being recorded, knowing I could later be held accountable for each word I said. That I might say something wrong.

She seemed disappointed. "I just thought when I saw your photo and your name…"

White people. I laughed as good naturedly as possible. "My mom would love it, I'm sure, but no. Sorry." I knew my smile made people comfortable, a perk of removing the mask.

She picked her phone up off the table and swiped through a few screens. "Okay. Do you have a boyfriend?"

"Not at present." I smiled, trying to keep myself pliable, affable.

"But you're looking for one?"

Really? I spoke carefully, "I don't think anyone's much dating in the current climate." I laughed a little, but she didn't even crack a smile. I'd *love* a boyfriend and it had been two months since I'd even hugged a guy. Hugged my family. I missed touch like it was food. Didn't make her asking any less annoying. *Just get through this and you'll be living on this hilltop, writing notes from a turret.* Free AC. Maybe they'd let me swim with the kid in the pool. And hiking I didn't have to drive to.

She said, "We just want to make sure you're safe. You know? For us. For our family. It is a global pandemic, you do understand."

I said, "I have elderly grandparents I haven't seen since lockdown. I won't even go into my parents' house. I've been nothing but careful."

She blinked and looked at her phone again like I hadn't said anything. "What experience in childcare have you had?"

"As I mentioned in my letter," *Which I took two hours writing, did you read it? Or my resume? How many people are you seeing for this job?* "I'm studying childhood education in college and have put in two years-worth of hours in their daycare center. I'm trained in CPR and early education and have had a full year of classes on childhood behavioral sciences. Plus. I practically raised my baby sisters."

Her eyebrow went up. "Oh? Your mom have a lot of kids?"

I tried not to think too loudly, as she was looking at me with the intensity of someone who can hear thoughts. I took a breath so I wouldn't sound pissy. I said, "She spaced us, five years each. I have two younger sisters."

She had stopped listening the moment I even began to answer her question. She furrowed her brow and crossed her arms.

"One thing I want to make clear, *no* social media. We want to keep our child offline and out of the press's eye as long as we can. The public doesn't even know we have a kid."

Wow, that's a level of secrecy I didn't think was possible these days. This answer was easy, "There are rules about minors and social media when it comes to childcare, so this has always been my practice."

"Do you have Instagram?"

"Yes, but I'd never put a kid on there."

"The house either."

"Got it. Of course." *Damn.* I was kind of hoping to show off my new digs.

"You'll be signing a nondisclosure agreement the moment you start work here, and it's good for twenty years. The part about photography is in the contract."

Does this mean I have the job?

"Understood."

She nodded and scrolled down her phone. It chimed and she swiped and laughed and started texting. "Oh my God, no she didn't!" she said and fell into texting like I wasn't there. I sipped my water and looked around. My eyes had adjusted to the shade, and looked at the French doors right off the patio. I could see into the living room with its white walls and vaulted wood ceiling. The furniture behind the glass looked expensive and spare. I was dying to get a tour of this place.

Celine giggled at her phone for another ten minutes and I sat quietly. I had gotten a lot more patient with time in the quarantine. It wasn't a bad thing on this gorgeous sunny day to be sitting on this back patio with a phenomenal view waiting for the white lady to finish with her phone. Star jasmine wound up the column of the overhang and blew gently in the afternoon onshore flow. It smelled a bit like heaven. The day was cooling already, and the light changed as the marine layer moved in. I'd give anything for a backyard filled with family, a barbecue with cousins and neighborhood friends, but for now, this would do.

A dash of blonde movement behind the window put me on alert. My brain read it as a cat or a dog first but then his pink face smooshed up against the window and I met Story, who was making the most horrible expression.

I looked over at Celine, still cackling at her phone and I scooted over to the edge of the sofa. I made a horrible face back. He stopped for a long moment and leveled his blue eyes right at me with his mother's steady gaze. I changed my horrible face into this upwards grimace my mom taught me; she and I were the only ones in our family who could make a near V out of our mouths. I wiggled my eyebrows and amusement entered his eyes. He squealed and giggled. Four was a lovely age. They just start having imaginations, they're easily amused, and most important, they haven't learned how to be assholes yet.

Celine finally looked up from her phone and watched us for a moment. I changed my face back into a smile and the boy laughed again. With a flow of linen overalls, blonde hair and expensive products, I had two grown arms around me, squeezing. I gasped. It was the first time I'd been touched in eight weeks. I stood up suddenly and she stood with me, not letting go.

"Oh. Okay." I tried to step away, anything to not shove her off. Fortunately, the squeeze ended, and she said, "I knew it, I just knew it when I saw your name! Soledad."

Her pronunciation was like you'd expect. *Soul ee dad.*

"What?"

"You're the one for Story. It's meant to be. I don't even need to see anyone else." She squealed something between a whee! And an *eee!* And spun in circles, arms wide and I was hired.

I didn't have much to pack. Computer and one suitcase chock full of summer clothes. I left a lot back in my apartment, things like Docs and jackets and jeans that wouldn't be necessary in summer. I brought my Psych textbook to stay fresh for the fall semester. I brought a journal, as I'd been in the practice since this nonsense happened, mostly daily writings of longing for a way out of this, longing to see friends again, but still, it made me feel less horrible to write it down. I tucked in a photo of my family at Disneyland in the Before. We are hamming it up at the sword in the stone, Cinderella's carousel behind us. My dad is making a goofy face and pulling on the sword, my mom's hair still dark, my sisters are laughing. *If only they knew.* Even my smile is surprisingly free from fear or worry. So long ago last November. We looked so young.

The 15 grand I stood to earn this summer would more than keep my room for me until I returned in the fall. We were going back to school in the fall, right? The mayor had said two months quarantine, tops. We could beat this thing. I could have a life again.

There was a nondisclosure agreement, and it turned out that Celine was married to a Really Famous Actor and there was a reason Moby had sold Wolf's Lair anonymously. Because the new owner was the one and only Oscar-winning drama and action star James Famous (nondisclosure, folks.)

I knew I couldn't tell my mom because she would never keep her mouth shut, so I just told her he was a foreign investor in movies and made up fake names for both of them.

Full disclosure on the nondisclosure: everything in this story is true. The names have been changed to protect my own ass.

My parents needed their car, and I was going to be gone a few months, so I ordered an Uber. I set up a grocery delivery for my folks, telling them I'd pay the extra with what I earned this summer. Getting into a car with another human, especially one not known to me was downright terrifying. I made the Uber driver roll the windows down and I wore my N95.

I sat on the right side of the car, so when I saw the gray stone wall start outside my window, I poked my head out and looked up. We passed the rusty gate and the steep stairs that curved up into the wall and I reminded myself to find out where they came out above. Did they go into the house?

The driver dropped me at the main entrance. Everything felt different because I was going to there to live now. It was weird hoisting my luggage and standing there outside the gate. As the Uber backed away, I had a sudden sensation of being stranded. I squinted up at the gatehouse and saw that the building extended to the right. If I craned my neck, I could see what looked like a very modern balcony with glass panels rising over the stone wall that stretched out down the hill.

The gate kicked into action, and I jumped back, startled. Celine was right behind it, up close, no mask. I must have made a noise of alarm because she looked amused when she flashed her expensive smile and said, "Welcome." Once the gate closed, we did an about face and I followed her to the dark wood door in the gatehouse. That turret was mine!

It was so quiet up here, nothing but the sound of a breeze kicking leaves of bushes, and trees surrounding the property, and birds. So many birds. She opened the door and handed me a key. "Not like you'll need to lock it, but in case it makes you feel safer." She slipped inside the building, and I followed. We stepped into a terra cotta floored small entryway painted white and lined with wood paneling that looked very country manor. There was a dark wood stairway, stained the same color as the floors of the house, off to the left. The apartment was cool and smelled lovely. Celine's bare feet scuffed, smooth and pedicured (were people still doing that?) up the wooden steps. As we got to the top of the stairs, the space opened up, revealing a large room with gabled windows on the south side of the room, complete with a window seat. There was a window that ran the length of the opposite side of the room that looked onto the main house—the castle. The house seemed smaller from up here. Over in one corner, like it was laid out for a princess, was a double bed directly below the turreted ceiling. It was ridiculously comfortable with a giant quilt and fluffy pillows, all of it white. Off to the right was an enormous wood-floored living room with windows that overlooked the road below. Potted plants littered the balcony. That modern balcony was mine. The floorplan of this "apartment" was as big as my parents' house.

I was told the sheets were Egyptian cotton, although I wasn't sure how that was different from American cotton, but Celine made it sound like they paid a lot for it. The entire space smelled of cleaned wood, essential oils, laundered cotton, and no dust. It was expensive and lush. She left me there, saying, "Come down to the house when you're ready."

Compared to my modern one room apartment with a window that looked onto another Tru-coat stuccoed liver-colored building in Glendale, this room was all white paint, smooth clean wood, and natural light. There was central cooling, I had no idea where they put the ducts, but it worked. This would be a heavenly place to spend a summer.

I put some of my stuff away, but then washed my hands, and locked the door with a key I'd put in a tiny shoulder bag where I stored my cell phone. I had my mask on, because despite Celine's maskless face, I didn't know how to be.

I walked toward the house across the driveway, which seemed steeper than when I'd first come here. The pavers were heating up already in the sun, but the air was still cool and beachy from the morning's onshore flow. A breeze rustled the wall of cypress trees that lined the property and they bobbed and swayed like ladies gossiping. It smelled wonderful.

I walked around the back of the house which took longer than I'd remembered the first time. The house now seemed bigger, like its scale was a shifting thing. I was to use the back door off the swimming pool. Even on this beautiful day, no one was outside. The pool filter knocked and bobbed, and a cluster of birds cheeped raucously somewhere in the brush beyond. The quarantine had brought quiet, but even the slowest day in Glendale couldn't match this idyll.

I approached the French doors at the back and knocked tentatively on the glass. The smacking of little bare feet on wood brought Story running to the back door. He stood there a moment staring up at me, squinting. I waved. He gave me that Celine stare and did not move.

I tried the doorknob gently and his face went from placid to terrified. Then he screamed. Bloody murder. Top of his lungs. It startled me so badly, I realized it had been a while since I'd been around kids. If I was still working daycare, it wouldn't have fazed me.

Celine rushed up behind him and scooped him up in her arms, which startled the scream into stopping and she opened the door, saying, "Come in." She scowled and put the boy down abruptly. She said nothing to me and rushed out of the living room waving her hand behind her, dismissing us both. Story looked after her, bereft.

I immediately knelt down to the kid's height and took off my mask. It was the first time I had been so close to a human face mask-free, and a panic came over me, but I breathed into it. This was the bargain. I had tested negative, I moved my life here, and we were mask free. Story was doing that four-year old open-mouthed breathing with a bit of drool. It had been a while since I'd smelled kid.

This family is safe. I reminded myself.

He had tears in his eyes. I said, "You scared me, you know." This surprised him. "I've never heard such a scary scream." His face relaxed a bit and he smiled. I said, "I'm Sol. We're going to hang out together this summer."

He said, "Soul?"

"It's short for Soledad"

"And you have a soul."

I laughed. Kids always bring the creepy. "Okay. Yep. I pretty much do."

Story was an imaginative kid. Relatively easy going. A bit whiny, but when his folks weren't around, I just used the old "That voice hurts my ears, can you ask me in a nicer way?" trick and it went away. James Famous didn't seem to be around, but I thrilled that he was in the same building. I wasn't a superfan or anything, but there was definitely a time in my adolescence when I crushed on him hard. Now I got to play with his kid all day.

That first day, Story and I colored. We drew. I read to him. I read *with* him which was nice. He was content for long periods of time leafing through a stack of books while I read my schoolwork. When I talked to parents, I always stressed the importance of quiet in a kid's life. Now it seemed like the year had brought it to all kids everywhere.

At lunchtime, Celine passed through the kitchen for a drink from the fridge. I asked her about hikes. She didn't seem alarmed by the request and said we were welcome to go, we just had to watch out for coyotes.

I made a mistake when I laughed a little and said, "I got it, but they're everywhere here. Never had trouble with one yet."

Her demeanor changed from mellow to urgent and her eyes got wild when she leaned in too close to me and said, "They seem small, but they hunt in packs. You see just one, you scare it away, you hear?"

"Of course…" She didn't smell good. Like the expensive products were there but she had an unbathed smell about her.

She said, "Don't let them see your fear, or they surround you and…" She must have read my incredulity because she trailed off and marched off to the front hall closet. I followed. She got out a long ginormous wooden staff, a walking stick. "Do. Not. Leave. The house without this." She handed it to me. It was thick and heavy, like something Gandalf would carry. I staggered, grabbing it with both hands. I wasn't expecting the weight.

I said, "I've been trained. I know how to scare off a coyote." I lied, but seriously, unless you were walking a small dog you were totally fine. They were here first, they eat small animals, that's how I was raised. A few loud noises and sudden moves and they'd run.

"If you leave the house with Story, you take this." She looked at me with an intractability. There was no way this was an argument that I could win and the humming of her actual fear beneath the command made me comply. There was something off in this woman's eyes.

I said, "Got it." I acknowledged by raising the stick I'd been handed.

LA is the most beautiful city, the mountains and hills run throughout, and their unstable geological makeup means that a lot of them haven't been built on. In much of the city, particularly close to hills, you were as likely to come across a family of deer as coyotes crossing your path, or skunks rooting through your garbage, as you were to hit traffic on a freeway. Nature coexisted with us here, always threatening to take over. Since the lockdown, traffic had subsided so much that the air was cleaner than it had been in any June past and there seemed to be five times as many birds. Or were we noticing them more? My friends posted pictures of bioluminescence coming back to Santa Monica Bay, for the lack of heavy tankers cruising through. I'd always said that given a year, nature would reclaim the city and everything I saw in these quiet months was proving this true.

After his afternoon nap, I packed Story's little backpack with organic wholesome whatever reconstituted rabbit food snax and filled his metal water bottle. When I asked Celine if she minded us hiking for a few hours, she waved me away. For a family that seemed to spend a good deal of money on this kid, they didn't show as much care as I thought they would. I heaved the anti-coyote stick and, with Story outfitted with his little backpack and masked up, we started out. There was a path right next to the house that ambled down the side of the hill. Story walked ahead singing something to himself. Four-year-olds have a constant stream of nonsense in their heads. It was nice to hear again. He scrabbled around a twist on the steep path quickly and I followed carefully behind, the cumbersome stick making things extra awkward.

"Stay close, okay?"

He said something back through his mask but soon disappeared behind a curve of brush.

"Story, wait for me at the bottom, okay?" I realized I didn't know this path yet, and if I was supposed to use this giant stick to protect this kid from coyotes, maybe I should be the one going first. I knew it was pretty damn unlikely coyotes would be interested in this noisy kid and his fumbling companion, but still, I jog-skidded down until I saw his little blonde head peeking from around a bush. He was very still, only his hair ruffling in the breeze. The smell of baking fennel, eucalyptus, and pine matched a distant onshore smell of ocean, making me think you really could buy paradise. I've visited plenty of beautiful places all over this city, but these people lived here. Some day I'd be hiking with my own kid like this—okay after college, after grad school where I'd likely meet my future husband, after I'd worked at a preschool and gotten maybe a PhD so I could set up my own school. But some day. And my kid would be a hiker. No question.

Story's mask swelled and sucked to his face with his breathing, reminding me of a ventilator. These days were filled with images of medical horror and its echoes were everywhere.

I said, "Hey, you. Hang on there a sec, I don't know this trail."

He waited. I was surprised by his stamina, he didn't even seem to be breathing heavily. I saw that the trail wound through the chaparral to the right and to a wider path on the left. I followed Story. We could try the path to the left another day. This was a project we could work on, mapping this place. The path rippled and wound and then went down sharply. The hillside was dotted with postmodern mansions, all glass, facing the water. Someone had hung a giant deflated mylar heart in their window. For the frontline workers. That was nice. I almost ran over Story who had gotten to the bottom of the path that came out on a road. I knew it was the circle around the reservoir, but knowing the length of the hike back up, I turned him around and we started to climb.

We got back to the house as it was reaching evening, and when we approached the back door, Story squealed "Daddy!" and ran to the door, fumbling with the knob a little too long and dashed through into James Famous's arms. It was an odd thing, seeing someone you'd watched in so many movies—a man you'd fallen for in his first romcom, felt bad for as he lost comrades in WWII, cheered for as he took down a drug ring, wept for as he mourned his tragically dead wife—take his four-year-old son in his arms. I felt suddenly privileged to know Story, who was so beloved by this icon.

I'd had to pee for about an hour now, so I approached as quietly as I could, hoping to slip past the living room when I was stopped.

"And this is Soul?" James Famous's voice thrummed through me, and I told myself to calm the fuck down. Was I thirteen or some shit? Actors are shallow and callous, this is what you learn growing up in this city. People in Los Angeles are jaded and unimpressed. It is how we LA. Okay, except for my mom, but still.

I turned and mustered my biggest smize. Then I remembered myself and took off my mask. Was it like a hat? The polite thing to do? My hands burned with the knowledge they had yet to be washed, but I reminded myself we were only exposed to coyote and deer germs, not COVID.

"Hieee....It's short for Soledad. Nice to meet you." I nodded to him, waved, and hung back which is what stood in for an outstretched hand these days.

He barked a laugh that was downright infectious and my heart beat like a teen fan. "Ah, Sol, that makes more sense." He didn't sound quite as gringo when he said my real name, or maybe I was still thrilling to that famous voice. He was barefoot, wearing a pair of meticulously worn jeans and one of those effortless white linen shirts that likely cost a lot, not only to purchase, but to maintain.

Story, who was astride his dad's hip, pulled his face to him. "We didn't see any coyotes, but we saw a SNAKE."

"A lizard, it was fast." I interjected.

"A SNAKE and it coulda killded us!"

I cringed thinking of the thousand ways this kid could get me in trouble. James carried his boy out of the living room toward the front door. I stood for a moment, uncertain. Then I scuffled to catch up.

I said, "We were in no danger, I promise." This kid was not allowed to embarrass me in front of a film idol. *Shut up. It's a job. He's just a dumb actor.* Why was I such a starstruck dipshit?

Our path took us down the front hall around through a gorgeous dining room. It was hard not to stop and gawk, but I needed to make sure JF understood me.

—Listen, it's just easier from here out I refer to James Famous as JF, you understand. If I said Brad, you'd know exactly who I was talking about. Or Ansel. Or Ryan, but you know all those guys, and he wasn't it. But he was as famous as that. The how is more important than the who here.

We ended up in an airy state-of-the-art kitchen that was smaller than I'd imagined, but well laid out and lit up orange and white with the sun's remaining rays. There were white walls, slanted white ceilings and the metal encased French doors at the end were open, overlooking the gatehouse and the driveway lined with cypress.

JF lowered Story from his hip and flashed a charming smile. I mean, it was *really* charming. "Nice to meet you. Thanks for hanging out with Story here for the summer. You must be thirsty." He grabbed a glass and filled it with ridiculously clear ice cubes from the fridge door and then water.

He held it out to me. After two months in isolation, it was such a foreign feeling having someone hand me something. It took me a moment and I started to reach forward. JF's face turned suddenly to a snarl and he roared and STOMPED. I yelped.

Story said, "Daddy!!!" and squealed with laughter.

I blinked as my fight or flight took a moment to clear, but JF was laughing. He reached out and took my hand bringing it to the glass like I was infirm. He brought my other hand up. His hands were warm with a cold patch from the ice, and he was definitely not as tall as he was in the movies. His eyes were as blue as they had seemed onscreen, and there was a very pale trace of scar on his eyebrow I hadn't noticed in years of watching him twenty feet high in theaters.

I said, "I'm sorry, you scared the…I've had a very quiet life lately."

He was still laughing. "I know, I know, unfair, I'm sorry. You just looked so terrified. Cracked me up. Like *boogety.*" He shook his fingers and made crazy eyes like he had in that one futuristic movie where he played a rich guy on the edge.

He said, "So, how do you like the house, huh?"

"It's incredible."

"Right? These old Hollywood homes are nuts, right? Old man Wolf really had a thing for German castles. He went all out with this one. Hired Lautner for that very gatehouse you're sleeping in, and you know he was working against type."

"Who?"

Amusement crossed his eyes and made me blush with embarrassment for not knowing who.

"Lautner was known for postmodern homes in the forties and fifties, floating above LA with views. You know, the Goldstein house? The chemosphere?"

I nodded, pretending I understood. When people got all amped up on references outside your knowledge, unless you wanted a pursuant half hour of 'splaining, it was best to pretend. I wasn't sure if the conversation was hard because of isolation or if JF was just like the few other stars I'd met. There was no there, there.

The sun had set now and the lights in the kitchen snapped on. I thought they were automatic, it would be appropriate to this world, until I saw Story in the corner by the light switch. He had reached it with a spatula.

JF's eyebrows shot up. "Ah. Clever boy. Well, I'll leave you to it."

And like that, he turned heel and was gone. The room was quiet, and the absence of this man was as startling as his entrance. I breathed in and out, carefully. I had to eat something.

Story said, "Yeah. He's like that." He climbed into the breakfast nook on the opposite side of the kitchen at the back of the house. He said, "What's for dinner?"

Wednesday was "date night," whatever that meant in the quarantine. I sat while Story had a bath. I washed his hair. There were so many rules about being alone with children at daycare, I felt somewhat exposed being left alone with a kid who was totally naked. I thought briefly about liability and lawsuits, *Don't be alone with a child without another teacher or aide, and if you are alone, only with at least three other children. Do not let the child undress in front of you.* It was all written to look like it was about the protection of the kid, but it was really about: what can we get sued for? I quelled those fears. None of those rules that applied in daycare applied here.

Story sang to himself. I handed him a washcloth. "Wash your nethers."

"My what?"

I motioned to his crotch area, and he said, "Oh. You mean my *penis.* Why didn't you just say the word penis?"

He said penis about fifteen times before he was through and I realized each family's culture is different, so I laughed when he did, got him jammied up, and finally got him into bed. In my elaborate instructions, twelve pages printed out and left on my bed that first night, Celine had said for me to text her each night after this had happened. I wondered if his parents spent any time with this kid. And what did they do before I got there?

I hadn't been in many parents' houses, but it seemed odd to have such a young child on a completely different floor. I wondered if they had loud sex. Don't get me wrong, Story's room was gorgeous. It had been fashioned out of a library or something, and had giant arched windows familiar from the rest of the house and was painted just as white. The walls were lined with dark wood bookcases with built-in drawers. He had a single bed tucked into a cornice whose walls echoed the shape of the windows. It had been painted a midnight blue and was dotted with gold leaf stars. Plastic planets hung from his ceiling and his bookshelf was laden with picture books and toys. A metal globe of the moon and one of Earth stood on a high shelf, along with some worn books, no doubt from his parents' childhoods.

His father's two Oscars kept a row of stuffed monkeys company. It thrilled me to see the golden statues up there. It also seemed curious. Did this four-year-old have the context for an Oscar? How did JF talk about it? "My major awards," or, "These silly things don't mean as much to me as you do." The answers to that question would let me know a lot about these people.

Celine flowed into the room wearing some ridiculous drapey robe of varying colors of silk. A*mazing technicolor dreamcoat* came to mind. It was open over a simple white gauze slip dress. I'm totally sure these people shopped somewhere I had never been and likely would never be allowed.

She smiled at me and said, "Thank you." Which meant that I was dismissed.

I said, "See you tomorrow, Story."

"See ya!"

I did like this kid, so there was that. Maybe I could give him a brief bit of normalcy in the weirdness of his daily life. In the weirdness of the quarantine.

When I got back to my turreted apartment above the gate, I found it a little stuffy, so I opened the windows and spent some time cleaning up, moving myself in properly. I FaceTimed my mom and showed her the apartment.

She said, "Can you make this a full-time job?"

"What, you want me to be a nanny?" I was busting on her, she knew my plans.

"No, no, I know, but look at those floors!"

"Wait'll you get a load of the bathroom." I showed her the white bathroom, porcelain tub, 1930s deco tiles in green tones, the giant fluffy towels. "Check it, this is a towel rack that heats my towels for me."

Mom made all the appropriate noises. Then she said, "Tell me these people's names again, I want to Google them."

"Mom, I signed an NDA, plus they're not that interesting." Ugh, I hoped "Anonymous" held and there wasn't an internet trail on Wolf's Lair she could follow. If she found out it was JF I'd never hear the end of it. Plus, Mami raised me not to lie, and none of this felt good.

"If they're not interesting then you can tell me!"

"I love you Mami, I gotta go."

"Wait, show me again."

I gave her one more slow pan of the room and held the camera really close to my face with a quick, "I love you," and hung up before more badgering. I missed her hugs, the smell of her, and hanging out in her kitchen and cooking together like a hole in my heart, but she did make the pivot to remote badgering seamlessly.

I made up my mind to have a real bath that night. I didn't do that often, but new tub, new rules and I'd go back to worrying about living in drought country tomorrow.

There was some lavender and rosemary bubble bath which smelled downright decadent, and I sank into the tub more sore from hiking than I expected. At home I clocked five miles a day walking, but something about scrabbling down and up hills worked different muscles.

As I lay in the most ridiculous fresh-smelling sheets that night trying to go to sleep, I reminded myself of my luck. Employed in the quarantine. Not sick. Living with a family who was playing it safe. Living somewhere fancy.

My parents were safe, to an extent, at least Dad worked in the big open-aired local Home Depot. He was in management, so not as much customer-in-the-face action. He was pretty good about his mask and everything. He knew Mom was at risk. At least in this completely different atmosphere I wouldn't have to dwell on it. They'd be fine right? Counting luck again: I was working for a movie star my mom would absolutely die over. Stories to tell the kids one day. No boyfriend in sight, so no kids, but that would follow. This was hardly cuffing season in Los Angeles.

I'd been counting blessings daily since a severe tailspin about a month ago: kids in cages, tyrant president looking to steal another term, my dad's green card renewal backed up in red tape at a time when ICE was on the rampage, women's rights going away, cops getting more brazen in their killings, pandemic with near 100 thousand people dead in our own country…that kind of tailspin. The tailspin where hope left and despair set in and I assumed my parents and grandparents would catch COVID and die because of being brown and having family living with them who couldn't exactly stop working the front lines. My uncle couldn't quit being a mailcarrier even though people kept walking up to him and yelling about their packages and their relief checks in his face.

Tailspins weren't sustainable in the pandemic, who knew how long this would go on? At least in this vaulted-ceilinged room above a gate to a mansion, it finally seemed possible to keep them at bay. The biggest thing to be grateful for was that this was a three-month gig and then I'd have fifteen grand to put away for grad school. Not too shabby.

The next morning, I tried to build my routine. First: breakfast in my giant apartment. I had ordered groceries the first day I arrived, so it was easy enough to pop in my earbuds, fry up a couple of eggs in the kitchenette, and make some coffee in a tiny French press from home. I listened to some music, then caught up on some podcasts and sipped my coffee. When I was ready, I locked my little door and crossed the driveway, the air salty and fresh and gray, the birds noisy in the cypress.

Kids like schedule and nothing begs for schedule like the quarantine, so I knocked on Story's door by seven. I creaked the door open. He was fast asleep. The room was totally different in the day, bright and airy and sunlit from gothic window behind his bed. Some light caught my eye, playing along the darker blue wall to the right. I looked around for its source, a prism? A glass object or something? The light moved over toward the bed. Prisms had the pattern of their swinging, they moved because they had been set in motion. But this light hovered in the air, moved toward Story and something in my gut told me to step in and stop it? Catch it?

I stepped forward as the light played on Story's face. It moved, hovering on the wall next to his bed. Or I moved and its placement changed?

Story sat stock upright and looked at the light saying, "Oh, hi."

I said, "Good morning."

But he put his hand up as if to shush me, listening toward the light, cocking his head. "Mmm-hmm. Okay."

He hopped out of bed and walked up to me. He said, "Oh, hi." I realized his first hi wasn't for me at all.

He was wearing cotton navy blue pajamas with piping on them and with his hair tousled, he looked a bit like a 1930s movie star

"Um, who were you saying hi to?"

"Mrs. Wolf, she visits sometimes. I gotta pee." He popped sideways into his bathroom, and I heard the toilet seat go up and he peed. I gave him a moment.

The light was no longer there, but a patch of ice had formed in the lining of my stomach. Au pair, haunted castle. *Don't be stupid.* Kids his age had imaginary friends. They just did this. I knew this from all my childhood development classes. I knew this from creepy things kids at the preschool had been saying to me for years now. I knew this from the time my baby sister Graci got so obsessed with "Bloody Mary" that she was convinced the woman's ghost was haunting her third grade bathroom.

I breathed. I'd gotten weird in the quarantine was all. I called into the bathroom, "I'll see you in the kitchen, Story, okay?"

He was running the water in his sink while he brushed. I made up my mind I'd find a water conservation book. Or a book about drought and LA. But this was our first full day together. It was a day to observe.

I stepped out of his room into the hallway and the sound of sobbing echoed from an indeterminate place. It was a woman's voice, and given the arched ceilings in this place that displaced echoes, I wondered if it was Celine. There was something deeper and throaty about the cries though; they came from someone with a larger frame, a bit of volume to them. I stepped to the stairwell and up two or three stairs to see if I could tell if it was coming from the second floor, but it sounded further away. I stepped into the hall to listen. I did not want to get any closer to whatever this sobbing was. The noise was in front of me and then moved behind me. It sounded like it was coming from the walls. Weird house, probably a weird echo.

But a sadness had seeped into my chest. Like that ice that had formed in my stomach at Mrs. Wolf, the imaginary friend, *the imaginary friend, just an imaginary friend*, as if that ice had blossomed and seeped throughout my body and I was now I inexplicably sad. Like a great weight. Another tailspin?

No, this was heavier. I recognized it.

My mom said that I'm a "sensitive." That I can feel disturbances in the Force, if you will. I've always been overly empathic, but there are odd days where I'm happy as anything and sadness seeps in and overwhelms me. Like there's something in the air. The first time it hit me this bad was when I was thirteen. I sat straight up in bed in a cold sweat and cried out for my mom, the room spinning in this oppressive blackness. She calmed me down and I went back to sleep and the feeling had not lifted the next day. It turned out a Tsunami had hit Fukushima, Japan. The feeling didn't leave me for days and my mom was worried about me.

Since March, I'd been waiting for the shadow of the mass death we were experiencing to hit me in the same way. But all I felt so far was a numb hopelessness and pervasive anxiety. I guessed that's what the rest of the planet was feeling, so maybe it was the company? Someone to carry it with? Here in the hallway in this growing icy gloom was the first time since this all began, and the first time since that major earthquake in India killed tens of thousands of people, that I had this specific feeling in my chest. It disoriented me.

As quickly as the sobbing had started, it stopped, but the black weight lay in my chest as heavy as when it arrived. I forced my body down the hall to the kitchen. I would make the kid breakfast. This feeling would pass, it always passed, but I couldn't help thinking something awful was happening somewhere. Aside from the obvious.

Celine was sitting at the counter in the kitchen in very expensive yoga gear, no tears in sight. This should make me worry about the crying I heard, but I was distracted by a ridiculously good-looking Black guy with shoulder-length locs wearing similarly expensive yoga gear standing at the stove. I wondered what I'd walked in on. Also, what did *safe* mean with this stranger here? How many people was this family "safe" with? I reached into my bag for my mask but hovered before putting it on wondering what good manners were correct here.

Celine looked up and seeing my concern said, "Oh, don't worry, it's just Marcus." She grinned. "The universe brought him to us, and now you to us. Everyone is in place."

In place for what? There was no further explanation as she scrolled on her iPad, so I threw Marcus a questioning look. He said, "I'm the cook." They have a cook? He must have seen the question in my face because he said, "I'm tested weekly, see no one outside the family, do meal prep for lunch and dinner in the morning after breakfast." At least he understood the worry, the virus, even if Celine didn't. He said, "You want anything?"

I regretted my stovetop breakfast in my apartment. I just shook my head. "No, thanks."

This guy looked like he should have a *life*. What did isolating himself for this family do to his lifestyle? He definitely had some honeys somewhere in the city. And from what I could tell from his tight bod, a gym. No one stays in that good shape with weights in an apartment.

Maybe the crying had come from someone with him. Or from him. No, it was a woman's voice, that much was sure.

I wondered how many other people were going to pop up at this place. I'd just built up my confidence level with the family, but Marcus threw the reality of the other people he could be in contact with, and the fear of all that contact math back into the daily mix. We weren't supposed to be seeing *anyone*. And here I was, exposed.

I said, "Where do you live?"

He laughed. I liked his laugh, he was a warm guy, very immediate. You'd have to be for people to invite you into their home to hang out every mealtime. He said, "Down the hill aways, off Beachwood."

I coveted the apartments in that neighborhood which ran from the mountain all the way down to Franklin. 1930s buildings, quiet sidewalks, access to all these trails and hikes. It was superwhite, but not totally hipster. Most people worked in the industry, line producers, prop people, enough salary, but not ridiculous. Unfortunately, the crappiest studio apartments started at $2500/month, so it was out of the realm of possibility for me and another reason my few months here were such a treat.

"Marcus!" Story's little voice and slappy feet came running down the hall and he jumped into Marcus's arms. This lonely little boy did have some company after all. I was foolish to think otherwise.

But this virus, this supercontagious killer virus. I was standing here without a mask on, indoors, about four feet from someone I didn't know or trust.

Marcus said, "Hey, Storymcrory! How you doing?" The warmth and love in his voice zinged through me.

Story said, "Can you make the pancakes?"

I said, "*The* pancakes?"

Marcus flashed me a smile sideways smile. "He likes the turtles."

Marcus had what, maybe ten years on me? But he was the first male outside my family I'd seen in three months and aside from the movie star, the first male I'd been this close to in longer. The first mortal male, I guess. *Down, girl.*

"Nice to meet you, I'm Sol."

"Nice to meet you, Sol. Turtle pancakes?"

He said my name right! "I'm good, thanks."

Celine huffed as she got off the breakfast nook bench. She kissed Story and kissed Marcus on the cheek and sashayed out of the room.

My original worry that they were a thing came back. A house with a couple with a kid was one thing. A house with marital complications was another.

As if he read my thoughts, Marcus said, "Don't you worry about her."

I startled. I said, "Should I worry about you?"

He laughed and it filled the kitchen. I felt the least lonely I'd been since March 17th when quarantine began. I popped open the fridge and grabbed a La Croix. It always seemed like a mark of the rich: nonstop beverages.

I slid into the breakfast nook and listened a little more closely as Story yammered on. I listened for clues about the light, about Mrs. Wolf. About his weird little family. But he was telling Marcus the story about our hike and that snake that was really a lizard.

A plate with a single perfectly formed pancake turtle with raisin eyes appeared in front of me.

"Oh, I already ate." I looked up at Marcus who was already back at the stove.

He said, "We're just happy to have a real live, eating person in this house, aren't we, Story?"

Story said, "I'm going to eat a real live person!"

Marcus looked at me. "Movie stars live on dewdrops and sunbeams, but kids can't. I'm glad Story has someone to eat with. To model healthy eating habits." He raised an eyebrow pointedly.

Cowed, I reached for the syrup. I said, "This looks delicious." I hadn't even thought of that aspect of growing up with a movie star.

Story said, "Mulbicious."

We laughed. The darkness wasn't gone, but I'd pushed it down for a moment. This wasn't supernatural, nothing I'd seen was. This was a kid with a good imagination. The realness of pancake steaming with syrup, the sun coming through the window on my back, the extremely attractive guy at the stove, the dark feeling in my chest was a shade of its original potency. I was in a big house with a lot of windows and noises and light and two anorexics. I tuned out from Story a little and started scrolling through James Famous movies in my head to recall if I'd seen him eat or gain an ounce. I felt for Celine, who had to keep up with the Joneses, or the Courtney Coxes or Anne Hathaways.

The days started to do what days do when you schedule sameness. But sameness is good for kids. Story knew that morning hike was time for the hill path, the mountains and the lizards. We saw deer and the occasional coyotes. I talked a lot about coyotes with him and never used the stick for anything other than hiking. I told him how it was safe if there were two of us and we were noisy. How coyotes were here long before people were, that we'd moved into their backyard. Maybe I could stop his mother's phobia here. Story was most excited when we saw bunnies and chased them. I made sure to bring a bunch of snacks and water so we could spend as long as possible outdoors. That was really good for kids this age. After staying Safer at Home for a few months when I was afraid of people on the sidewalk, it was good for me too. After a few days I felt my hiking muscles kicking back in and my breath came back with my strength. It only took two days for that dark weight to leave me in my new outdoor life.

We went back home in time for lunch, left there by Marcus who always added a little drawing and a note for Story. That first day it was a picture of a snake towering over a cowering Story. He drew me with a stick raised against the snake. Cute.

After lunch we had reading time. If I'd worn him out sufficiently, Story would pass out right there on his ridiculously lavish window seat and I could catch up with friends online, and with the news. After a while I left the news for Mondays and Fridays. The doomscrolling was starting to wear, especially as so many people had died in New York and people in LA still weren't, for the most part, wearing masks.

As the hottest sun waned around 4:30, it was time for our down the street stroll. Both masked, we nodded at people as we passed. It was good to see other humans, even if we couldn't get close. We were together in our aloneness. We wound down the hill and, as the place was locked down, there were hardly any cars.

Then back to the castle for dinner. Story ate with his parents, and I got my break back in my little turret where I'd stream *Gentefied* or *Insecure* just to pretend real LA with all its people was out there happening like it used to. I ate something I microwaved, because by then I was too tired to cook. I came back down at eight when Story's parents dismissed him and went upstairs, to whatever they did up there, and I got him through his bedtime routine.

The flow of the days was a welcome change from the doomscrolling alone in my apartment in Glendale, my terrified trips to the supermarket at odd hours, and entirely too many hours alone. I would take this life, temporary though it was, because at least it felt something like living.

About two weeks into this routine, the days were hot, but the evenings were cool to chilly when the marine layer rolled in. It was mid-June and the days were longer. Story and I walked along the road on our evening neighborhood walk, and he'd found a stretch of curb along a curve of the hill. There was a drop off the other side, but it was a few feet out. It's what my instructors would call "an acceptable risk." Story was walking one foot on the curb, one off in super slow-mo. I looked up at a peculiar building that rose up the side of the mountain, with balconies facing outward, but its back against the beige rocky wall of hill. I tried to figure out if the building was apartments or a single home. And if it was a single home, what was that floorplan like? Would you sleep further up or have your living room further up? Was it single rooms with stairwells connecting them?

Story's concentrating on every other foot made him speak in stops and starts. "But it's the way we do things every…every day that makes me…feel icky and the same, the…same." Trust kids to nail it.

It was a house, I decided, but I blame that distraction for almost running into the woman. And if I hadn't?

"Oh, I'm sorry." She was wearing a mask, so that was a relief, but I instinctively moved between her and Story, whom she was staring at in a weird, fixed way. I looked at him. I dressed him reasonably for the hike in a white t-shirt and forgettable shorts. I didn't want him out in the open in the star kid artisanal weirdgear his closet was filled with. Who cares he was wearing Timberland sandals? Everyone up here was reasonably wealthy, so it wouldn't draw too much attention. Sixty bucks was not a lot for kids' shoes in this neighborhood.

The woman would not stop staring. Her eyes were iridescent blue, and her hair had been dyed black a few months back but was showing a dull brown in a distinctive line around her head. Hairdressers were definitely not for everyone these days, so I didn't judge, I just found her energy weird. She was simply dressed, jean shorts and a t-shirt. She wore Converse, which I liked, and judging by what little I could see of her face, seemed to be in her thirties.

But it was the *way* she was looking at Story that made me grab his hand.

She said, "Antonio?"

He stared back at her, that Celine stare, and I tugged at him a little.

"C'mon kid, let's head on home. See what Marcus has cooked up." I said the male name like casting a spell. *I am not alone with this child. We have a protector.*

There was something about this woman's intensity that made it feel like things could go suddenly sideways. She could grab him or shove him over the edge. The drop wasn't much, but if he was thrown it would become a plunge. She could…I didn't know. I took his hand and we headed up the hill. I was worried the woman would follow us, but she stood watching after us for a moment and by the time I turned back to see if she was still there, she was gone.

When we got back to the house it was getting dark. We washed up and headed into the kitchen. I shook off the strange lady, worried that if I brought her up, I'd jeopardize my position. Part of what Celine had talked about in her first day long-ass endless lecture was keeping Story "safe." She told me that JF had some threats on his life and they'd both had some fringe people get kinda obsessed with them and track down where they live. That's why they kept Story out of the news. They figured if they didn't say they had a kid, there'd be less of a chance of his being in any kind of peril. Wolf's Lair, sold anonymously only a few months before, was meant to keep their location anonymous…at least for the quarantine.

After she'd said that, I did a search on Story, on JF having any kids and found nothing. Absolutely nothing at all. Which was really hard to believe. Even the most protective parents couldn't seem to keep their kids' names and birth details out of the public eye. They must have hired someone to erase him. What money can buy.

I got Story to the dinner table and waited. The sun was still out, turning golden on the dark green hills beyond the roofline of my little apartment. We were headed into summer solstice, and I knew the cool days wouldn't last and the green hills would soon turn brown. We'd have to hike earlier, and I'd have to think of some sort of afternoon indoor activity to keep the kid occupied.

The family often ordered in food, sometimes Marcus left them salads in the fridge. But tonight, unlike every other night in the three weeks I'd been here, Celine did not float into the room, kiss her offspring on the head and slide into the breakfast nook with an intimate crinkle of her nose that made Story light up inside, aglow with a scant moment of attention.

I waited a few minutes, trying to listen for noise from upstairs. What did they do with themselves all day? Sometimes I could hear JF take a phone call. Celine laughed randomly once in a while, making me think she was texting someone. But how exactly did they spend their long days if not with their kid?

Story leaned on my arm and let out a *nnnnggggg* of complaint.

"You hungry?"

He nodded piteously. We did have quite a hike and this kid was busy growing. I said, "Me, too."

I moved over to the counter where bananas hung on a chrome banana tree. I'd only seen them in magazines. It was such an odd single use device. I plucked one off and was reaching for peanut butter in the cabinets when I felt someone's hands on my ribcage. After three months of quarantine the touch was so intimate and startling, I whipped around gasping and there was JF standing right behind me, so close I could smell his unbrushed breath, a faint smell of sweat, lemongrass soap.

He put his hands up, "Woah, woah, just wanted you to know I was behind you."

It was a narrow passage between the counter and the island. But people got that close in restaurants, they'd usually touch a shoulder, not your lower back or sides. They certainly didn't grab and squeeze. I was flushed and startled, and JF searched my eyes with his ridiculously recognizable ones as if searching for signs of life.

Story said, "Daddy!!!!" and ran into him full stop. I slid sideways past the two of them and fumbled for a spoon in a nearby drawer. If this fucker was going to turn creeper, I was out of here.

The lights turned on suddenly again at just the right time, and there was teleporting Story by the door to the kitchen. He said, "I'm hungry."

JF said, "Hungry for action!"

The look of worry and disappointment in Story's eyes made me think the hope of eating soon had disappeared for him. I grabbed a dish and said, "Story, let's make peanut butter boats."

JF's smile was frozen on his mouth and had left his eyes as if he were considering what to do. He said, "Yup, yup, peanut butter boats, I'm most curious."

Which is how I ended up sitting in a breakfast nook across from the most famous man in America as I scooped out tiny boat-sized bits of banana and put peanut butter on top of them to feed to his kid. And how we ended up in a peanut butter naval battle, laughing. And half an hour passed this way. JF wasn't a creeper, he was just a touchy guy. It happened again, I'd tell him I was uncomfortable, and he'd back off. Things were different in the post #metoo workplace. Right?

I said, "Um, is Celine coming down? Do you want me to get Story some dinner?"

I had somehow confused the father of this small child. "Oh, no, she's. It's a mood I guess you could call it. Yes, I imagine he'll need to eat." He turned his eyes, lit with mischief to Story, "Catch as catch can, bud."

Story looked like someone had told him it was Christmas morning. I said "What?" and he was up on his feet standing in the breakfast nook. I said, "Oh, okay," and he stepped over me, jumped onto the floor and skidded over to the fridge where he slid open the freezer drawer.

As he rifled through containers he said, "No, No, No. Pizza. Spaghetti!"

He pulled a labeled Tupperware out of the freezer, popped it into the microwave and with a few presses of the button dinner was on. It took only two minutes until the most delicious smell of garlic, oregano, and tomatoes filled the room. Clearly Marcus's magic. Story picked up the microwaved dish. "Careful, bud, that's hot," I said.

JF was sitting at the table looking into the distance, distracted while his four-year-old carried a tray of scalding hot food across the entire kitchen and lifted it onto the table. I caught the dish before it slopped onto Story. I wasn't sure exactly what to do, I hadn't lingered this far into dinner before. I slid out of the breakfast nook and said, "Well, I'll see you tomorrow."

"No, please, stay." JF's deep, solid voice echoed in the space. I'm not impressed by fame, but there was something about such a plaintive request coming from a man I'd been through the wars and murders with. It took me a moment to remember myself, and it was even more awkward to break the silence that followed.

I said what I thought I was supposed to say, "Celine said, meal time is family time."

He laughed hollowly. He said, "Yes she did, but she's not here, is she? Celine has…days. It's always hard to keep her happy." He ran his hands over his face. "Lord knows I try. I do *everything* to keep her happy. You would not believe the lengths I go to." His eyes flickered briefly over to Story and then back to me. "It's never enough." I waited an uncertain moment, unable to think of an appropriate response. Did he not want to have a kid? Damn. The less I knew about this marriage, the easier my job would be.

He said, "Sometimes she just needs her space." Then, as if the spell had broken, he said brightly, "Please, grab yourself a meal, there are plenty in the freezer. *Marcus* makes sure of that." The way he emphasized the name Marcus made me think my suspicions were correct.

My stomach grumbled as if in answer. At least food would be a prop to cut down on the awkwardness of all this. I headed over to the fridge. "You want anything?"

"No, thank you. I ate."

Sure you did. When I left Story with them for dinner every night, did they sit opposite him with no food, or did they use other anorexic tricks like pushing food around their plates? I wondered if I could undo the damage of his parents not eating dinner in the time I spent with Story for breakfast and lunch.

That spaghetti smelled so good, I got my own and popped it in the microwave. I grabbed a blood orange Pellegrino from the fridge to make it fancy. The microwave ticked along, and everything became a bit too quiet for three people in the room. I said, "So, how'd you two meet?"

JF launched right in, his delivery measured and rehearsed. "I met Celine on the set of *Beirut with Love*. She was a makeup assistant, and once I saw her, we clicked, it was all over."

"It was all over," echoed Story.

"She's my best friend, my confidante, and she keeps me laughing."

The microwave beeped echoing in the kitchen, only punctuating the fact that laughter was something I didn't hear much of in that house. I also knew that I had read this exact wording somewhere in a *People* or *OK! Magazine* at my mom's house or in a salon. *Remember hair salons?* This guy was speaking PR at home and at that very moment any admiration for him, starstruckness, thrill of proximity vanished into pity. If you are what you do, and you couldn't do what you did because of the pandemic, and your wife of fifteen years has "days," and maybe you didn't even want a kid, what kind of life was this for their son?

If we ever got out of this I would build a real life. With real people. And if I had a kid I'd spend every minute I could with him and if I left him with someone else it would be family. Because this, this was just weird.

"That's great." I couldn't really think of a more complex answer for this PR portrait of the marriage, so I turned the talk back to Story. I said, "Good choice, Story, this smells delicious!"

Maybe I was too animated, because Story eyed me warily. I said, "You like it?"

He nodded, spaghetti still sticking out of his mouth. He sucked it in with a noisy slurp leaving sauce all over his face. He laughed. His father laughed. I laughed a little. I made up my mind right then not to be caught alone with these two again. I was handling enough on my own, I couldn't absorb the heady sadness that was filling this space…the sadness I'd picked up on earlier in the afternoon. I'd make a bubble for this sweet boy. He deserved a fun bubble in all this until he could return to school.

I looked up at JF who had transformed into Sad Dad. He was watching Story with a kind of helplessness. Was that a tear? Was this a performance for me?

It had been a while since I made small talk. The quarantine had brought on long quiet hours, lots of zoom conferences for my classes as my teachers "pivoted," some less successfully than others. I had done a lot of staring into space. My days used to be so structured around getting to and from classes, finding places to eat, working in the library. But when everything stopped it felt like my brain did, too.

They say that kids who sit down to dinner with their parents every night are more likely to succeed in school and are less susceptible to mental illness or the call of drugs. I'm not sure this scenario of Sad Dad not eating while his kid slurped microwave spaghetti was what *The New York Times* had in mind when they came out with the article. Maybe when Story was working his way through rehab, he'd remember me in the dim recesses of his mind.

Damn, that dark was rising again. I fended it off by asking JF, "So, what did you get up to today?"

He looked at me, truly offset by the question. As if he were sifting through his head to make up an answer. He paused and said, "You know, the usual, reading scripts, making phone calls. Running lines."

"What, is anybody shooting now?"

"No, just gotta stay sharp you know." His voice was hollow, defensive.

I had nowhere else to go, conversationally, so I started asking questions about my favorite movie he'd worked on. I knew he had a rapport with the cast, and I'd read an interview, so the questions were comfortable and the answers pre-scripted and the conversation became easier. As I saw Story relax, I knew it was worth the extra effort.

And, because JF was here in front of me, because I was curious and because I was running out of topics to bring up, I said, "You guys have done a really good job at keeping Story out of the media."

JF looked up suddenly and sharply at me, stared a moment and then put on a calm smile. As if he had physically applied it to his face like a mask. "We go to great lengths. Why, what'd you find?"

"Nothing at all, like I said."

For a man who'd never been interviewed about it, he certainly did seem prepared, "Well, it's always been important to us that Story have a normal life, a normal childhood. We don't want my fame to alter his experience of childhood in any way."

Says the man living in a castle above a city about a child who has no other children in his life.

I nodded, trying to keep my face as pleasant as possible. I looked at my spaghetti in case it wasn't coming across honestly. Again, Mami did not raise me to lie, so it didn't come easily. "Well, that's really great." *Great. Find another word.* "What are you going to do about school?"

"What do you mean?"

"Pickup, drop off, his name."

He laughed suddenly and nervously. "We don't exactly have to worry about that now, do we?" I guess my incredulity came across. He said quickly, "We'll figure it out. But in the meantime, he's just a kid, right?"

I had to pull my lips back from my teeth with conscious strings. "Right," as I wondered why he looked so distressed about that.

I crept back to my apartment that night determined to let go of this family for just the evening. I sent like five goofy memes to my sisters, and they responded but they were sixteen and eleven and too busy for much interaction. I was processing too much to have any sort of honest conversation with my mom. I guess this sudden rescue of relocation ending up weird had disappointed me, knocked hope down again. With that and that heavy feeling this morning, things just seemed harder tonight.

I had season three of *Orange is the New Black* on Netflix. If I had to go to prison to be near real people again, so be it. The quarantine had done this to me. I had two friends I kept in touch with but everyone else had, in the great hunker down, fallen silent. Tastee, Suzanne, and Flaca were instead of company. Someday we'd be out of this. Right? In the meantime, I'd chip away at my degree, and binge Netflix in my turret.

I grabbed a shower and popped some microwave popcorn. Comfort food. I curled up in the lush white robe that had come with the place and turned on my computer. I was halfway into episode six when the lights flickered, and I heard an animalistic screech that cut through the room and into my bones.

I jumped out of bed, my feet hitting the floor with a solid *thunk*. I looked around the room…nothing. I peeked out the window at the house, which stood there quietly. JF and Celine's bedroom light on. Story's off.

I don't think you can imagine sounds that intense, but maybe…

It was like that feeling when you wake up during a fast earthquake…part of your sleepy self wonders if it happened at all. I sat on the bed and waited a moment. The next screech had me pull my knees to my chest to get my feet off the floor. It was in the room, surely. Or.

I stood again and moved over toward the stairs and turned back to face the room to see, hear better? When the screech came a third time, it was definitely coming from down the stairs. Clearly a wild animal had gotten into the house. I scuffled over to the coyote stick, which was leaning against the bed. I slid into my sneakers, grabbed the stick, and started stepping down the stairs, slowly.

There was no noise aside from the ever-present echo of crickets.

The third time it came from under the stairs. I looked along the wood paneled wall in the entry that I'd passed at least three times a day in the weeks since I'd been here. I knocked on it and found it hollow. I knocked the panel next to it, which sounded like there was solid wall behind it. I pushed my hands over the surface of the hollow panel, and down to a scuff in the wood where I found a very small keyhole. I knocked on it with the stick and the sound reverberated, answered by another ear-splitting screech. I breathed heavily, and, in full knowledge of the weight of that stick, I pushed on the panel, and it swung open. Of course, the door creaked. There was a light switch outside that I had tried a few times when I moved in, and I'd figured it went to something that wasn't there. I turned it on now and it mercifully lit up the dark cavern beyond the doorway in which I stood.. That dark cavern turned out to be a wood paneled, perfectly adorable circa 1940s hidden tiki bar. I walked in immediately. Olden 1940s era blonde wood paneling ran along the ceilings and walls, and recesses in those walls held paintings, classic colonialist tropical island exploitation art. A leopard patterned sofa ran alongside a wet bar made of rattan, and similarly covered bar stools lined it.

I had to laugh.

A shriek, up close this time and painful to the ears, stopped that laugh quickly. There was a scrabbling behind the rattan bar, and I brandished my stick and hoisted myself up on my stomach leaning over the edge to see. The noise was too loud for a rat. Something scrambled just out of my reach, rattling the rattan and knocking bottles as it did so.

I leaned away breathing heavily, but reminding myself wildlife was rampant in LA, this was no more startling than the opossum I'd caught in the dumpster out back of my apartment building, and was certainly less scary than the skunk I'd encountered at my parents' house. Did opossum make noise?

This was some kind of infestation. This was not my job. I'd tell them about it in the morning. They could get animal control out here or something. I whacked the bar threateningly with the club three times, hoping the thing would cower instead of getting out into the apartment. I scooted out and closed the door behind me, Maybe whatever it was would settle down for the night or get out the same way it had gotten in.

I was too amped up to go back to bed, so I stepped outside the door into the courtyard. The air was thick with marine layer and the sky was orange with light pollution. I breathed deep and inhaled fennel, eucalyptus, and the faint smell of cypress, as the gardeners had trimmed the trees. The marine layer acted like a blanket, holding in the sound of crickets and distant traffic and helicopters. The demonstrations against police violence were still happening in Hollywood, but in this strange, quiet space, crowds of people, scuffles, all of it seemed far, far away. Nothing touched you if you were rich enough.

It was ridiculous here. I walked across the driveway along a wall covered by a pink jasmine vine. I wouldn't be here in February when it bloomed but it must be quite spectacular. Voices murmured from around the side of the house. I walked toward it, knowing the corner of the house blocked me from view.

JF's voice cut clearly through the night air. That lid of the marine layer made everything a bit louder. "I don't know what you want from me, Celine. I've done everything, everything for you." He was playing the role of a plaintive lover. But no one is that good an actor.

Celine's voice was harder to make out—she was the murmur. JF's got louder. I realized from the sound of the bobbing filter that they were sitting by the pool. I inched up to the edge of the house around the corner from them. Maybe I could figure out what was up with Celine, learn some way to frame it for Story. I peeked around the corner and saw Celine was sitting on the edge of a chaise lounge, JF pacing in front of her.

He said, "We can't. My career would be over. And you. We don't even know what they'd do to you."

In the quiet of the quarantine, I wondered at how many conversations supposedly private were being overheard across the city.

She said, "I didn't think it would be like this."

JF said, "We have a nanny," I bristled at the term. I was an au pair, this was a summer gig. He continued, "You finally have me grounded, home with you, every moment. Still you're not happy."

She moaned something into her hands.

JF said, "Goddamnit, I know it's bad for everyone, that's not what I was talking about. I just mean, if we're going to be stuck here, can you work, can we work at enjoying it? Story's a pretty cool little dude, we could…"

"*What* exactly? Go to the park? Go to Disneyland? Take him on the red carpet?" This pandemic was hard on all kids, I guess, even stars' kids. Celine spoke clearly and there were tears in her voice. JF sank to his knees in front of her, looking up into her eyes with tears in his. Real life as Oscar material.

He said, "All you ever wanted to be was a mother. And look, you are! Story's a miracle, he's your miracle. You said so. You knew he was yours the first moment you laid eyes on him."

I wondered if he was adopted or these were just new agey weirdos; every kid a journey. The kid's name would argue new age. JF buried his face in Celine's lap and she crumpled over him, murmuring into his hair. I backed away from this scene, guilty I'd even gone to eavesdrop. There was some real shit between these two and it wasn't any of my business. I knew with some shame that my excuse about helping Story was bullshit.

All families have drama and I've seen some things from parents at pickup I wish I hadn't, but this was something else entirely.

The next morning, I was groggy since the adrenaline from the animal intrusion and weird bosses kept me up way too late. I woke Story and when I was gathering some of his things, I ran into JF in the living room. In a way, I was relieved to see him sitting there doing something normal like reading a script, using a normal part of the house for a normal purpose, not cruising through the kitchen, or lurking around upstairs.

"Hi," I said when he looked up.

"Morning."

"Um..." if I brought it up now, I wouldn't have to text Celine about it. "I think there's an animal in the guest house. "

He stared, his big blue eyes blinking with a blankness that indicated he was either frightened or every single thought had left his head.

I kept on, "There was this screeching noise and when I went downstairs— you guys never told me about the secret tiki room." I added the last part quickly, anything to take that creepy blank look from his eyes.

He grinned at that and nodded, "Pretty cool, huh? Speakeasy days. Old man Wolf had some parties in there."

"Yeah. Cool. Only I went in there and there was another screech, like high pitched, painful. And something was scrabbling around in there."

Something clicked in his eyes, and he turned back to his script. "Yeah, that's Missy."

"Um. Who?" Did they keep an animal down there?

"She's a ghost. Mr. Wolf's gibbon." He said it as flatly as if he were listing what he was wearing.

"A…gibbon…ghost?" Gibbon was a monkey, right?

"I'm sorry she scared you. Not everybody can hear her. Apparently, we can't do anything about it. It just comes with the castle. Doesn't bother us in here…so…" He shrugged. *Shrugged.*

"The *ghost* of a monkey?" He looked at me with his steady blue eyes and I wasn't sure if he was just messing with me, like when he scared me in the kitchen. Guys like him were always messing with you and guys like him usually didn't believe in ghosts. I didn't know any other way to ask a question. I said, "Are you making fun of me?"

His expression turned to annoyance. "The place is haunted. It's just noise, not a big deal. I'd rather have the screeching gibbon than the weeping Old Lady Wolf we have in the big house."

That crying I'd heard. It wasn't Celine? Or was he trying to distract from Celine? I said, "Mrs. Wolf? Why does she cry?"

"I don't know. Maybe old man Wolf was a real jerkoff. She divorced him, moved out, that's public record. If she ended up here again, that would suck."

"I'm sorry?" This guy's operational reality was so different from mine I felt like we were having different conversations from each other.

An edge crept into to his voice, he said, "I don't really understand what the problem is. Celine already tried burning sage."

Ugh. My bruja Auntie would have a thing or two to say about that. White people were always messing with powers they knew nothing about.

If these people talked so freely about the dead family that once owned this place, that totally explained Story's imaginary friend being called Mrs. Wolf. I stood there waiting for some further explanation and JF looked up at me impatiently, like, *are you done?*

I walked back to the kitchen. Monkey ghost-believing non-eating weirdos lived here. Or maybe ghosts lived here. Fine.

It was like most of 2020. Someone would tell you something preposterous, like people were injecting bleach into their bodies to kill COVID because the president suggested it. And you'd have to absorb the information and move forward. *Okay then.* Pivot. Move on with your day.

On the third day that Celine didn't join us for breakfast or dinner, I asked Story, "Is your mom okay?" I knew the answer, but I kind of wanted to know where he was with all of this strangeness.

He looked at me a curious moment with his face scrunched up. "What do you mean?"

"I haven't seen her in a few days." *Oh god, she got COVID and they're not telling me. I've been exposed and they're not telling me.* This was a 2020 phenomenon too. I'd have a day where I just felt comfortable and thick fear rose up suddenly.

He went back to his blocks, saying, "Mrs. Wolf says she's just having a hard time abjustin. Ajustin. A."

"Adjusting? To?"

He drove his toy car up the bank of a triangular block and launched it into the air, slo-mo, "To life as a mother."

Damn. This kid. And his psychoanalyzing imaginary friend? And how long does one have to adjust if it's been four years?

There was nothing different about our hike, or our conversation as we climbed the hill back to the house that evening, but I asked Story a question, he looked back to answer, and he skidded. He fell forward and his head hit a rock with a meaty *crack* I will never be able to unhear. I got to him in moments, and he was heaving, that deep crazy breathing before the wail starts. The blood took a moment, but it started flooding. My first aid training kicked in and I pulled my mask off my face and pressed it to his forehead. He started wailing. I knew with kids that you had to allow them to calm down before gauging the seriousness of the injury. I looked at him, worried but as unalarmed as I could, saying, "You bumped your head, that was hard. I know that hurts. *Shh. Shh.* Yeah, that's the worst. I'm sorry bud. Let's get you back to the house." I continued talking at him until he calmed down to minor sobbing. I said, "Do you think you can get up?"

The moment he got to his feet I saw he was wobbly, which is not what you want to see with a head injury. His sobbing had become a hiccup and I kept the pressure applied as best I could as we stumbled down the hill. I felt exposed, my face out in the open like that and prayed we wouldn't run into other hikers. Jesus, we had to get him to emergency, this was awful.

As soon as we got to the house, I tried texting Celine as I'd been instructed to while in the house. But there was no response. I shouted at the bottom of the stairs.

"Hello? It's an emergency!"

No answer. I should just call 911, but maybe it wasn't a 911 thing. Fuck the rules, I was going up those stairs. I turned to Story, who was clamping his hands over mine still holding my mask to his forehead. I said, "Can you hold this to your head for a minute while I get your mom and dad?" He nodded, tearstained, bloody, and grubby.

The stairs were a gentle slope of dark wood with a carved wooden bannister that ran up to the pristine white hallway at the top of the stairs. There were four doors at the top of the hall. I imagined, based on the noise, that the one at the far end was the bedroom. I crept toward it, when I heard some yelling.

Celine said, "Are you kidding? This will RUIN you. Do you understand? RUIN."

Oh shit, did James Famous get cancelled?

His voice was lower, more sonorous and harder to make out, but he said, "What's right..."

Hmmm. Moral dilemma on a guy I hadn't seen stand up for anything since I got here.

Celine's voice was high with anger, and clear, "What the fuck do you know about right? You were fine with it when I told you."

"I wasn't fine with it, it was too *late*. You knew that." There was so much rage and desperation in this, but I stepped forward before I heard more, before they heard me hear more, because Story was bleeding downstairs and we had to take him to get some stitches.

I went back to the stairwell and made my footsteps fast, loud, and steady toward the door where I knocked loudly.

Celine swung the door open so quickly it startled me. She had been crying, for quite some time from what I could see. She was furious, but then saw my bloody hands and shirt and my face. "Oh my god, what happened?"

"Story fell and knocked his head and it's bleeding a lot. I think we have to take him to emergency."

Usually noncommittal JF sprung off the bed like a papa bear, shoved his wife aside, pushed past me and galloped down the stairs. Celine followed him hollering, "We can't go to an emergency room. It isn't safe."

They weren't wrong. The numbers of COVID cases were up, and the amount of time you'd have to wait, it wasn't going to work at all. But this kid. They had to get a CT scan at least.

By the time I got downstairs to the front hall bathroom, JF was pulling the skin apart on Story's sobbing forehead and I swear I saw skull. He grabbed a towel off a rack and said, "Okay, buddy, I got you, I got you. Sol." He barked, but one thing daycare taught me, anxious parents aren't the kind of thing you can control.

I got to him as quickly as I could. He said, "Hold this, apply pressure." Sometimes you gotta let freaked out guys tell you the things you already know. There was so much blood. Faces bleed a lot, time in the playground will teach you that, but a lot is a lot. Celine swayed behind me, helpless about what to do. Story was watching her through his tears.

She said, "Story, how did this happen?"

At that he wailed. He'd been crying, but he wailed completely. I put my free arm around him and hugged him hard while he sobbed, keeping my hand pressed to his forehead. "Shhh, shhh…we're going to get to you a doctor and he'll patch you up."

JF's voice echoed in the hallway behind, calling out in a tense, false cheer, "You don't need a doctor, do ya buddy, it's just a little nick. We'll fix that right up."

I said, "I really think we should get him stitches, a CT scan." Concussions can sneak up on you, and we always erred on the side of caution at the daycare. His skull had smacked *hard*. If there was an internal bleed…

JF was behind me so quickly, it made me jump, then he was kneeling on the floor next to Story, way too close to me, lighting a candle. He held a needle over it.

"What the hell are you doing?" I instantly knew I should have reworded it but, damn.

He smiled at me confirming in the same way his cop self had when he took the wheel of a boat, only instead of "I trained in the navy," he said, "I got EMT training for that 9/11 movie."

"*The Second Tower*?" But EMTs don't give stitches, they patch you until you can get to a doctor.

He said, "I got this, don't I buddy?"

The actual fuck?

Out of an emergency bag he yanked a bottle of antiseptic spray, took off the lid with his hand and sprayed it. "Lidocaine, it'll numb him."

"Only on the surface, Jesus, do you…"

He looked at me. "Now move out of the way and let me take care of my son."

He held the needle up and went in and Story's scream ripped through the house. I watched Celine as she chewed on a nail and stood back. There was a flash of light off…a window? No, off a wall, and it moved slowly, hovering behind JF. When Story locked eyes on it, his wailing stopped, and he quieted to sobs. Mrs. Wolf. Definitely not imaginary. He sniffed.

"Good little man, just one more."

Story murmured, "Mrs. Wolf says…"

"I need you not to talk, buddy, okay? Just for a minute. You can tell me all about it when I'm done."

The second stitch produced a high-pitched keening from Story, but no scream. That noise reached into me more deeply than the prior one and I wanted to hit JF. I bit my lip and stood very still. This was ridiculous. I wanted to grab him and take him somewhere, get him away from this. But not my kid, this wasn't my kid. Not my call.

Celine said, "Brave, brave boy. There's my boy. My baby. We don't have to go to the emergency room. All that waiting? All those germs? Daddy can patch you up right here at home."

Ugh, these people. They weren't wrong. It's just. I had my lifeguard training. I knew we'd have to keep him up that night for at least two hours. Check his pupils…

JF ran a flashlight in front of his eyes.

I was a kind of freaked out, so I spent the night in Story's room. I kept him up two extra hours and then woke him periodically to check his eyes. That purple light reappeared somewhere around eleven, hovering over the bed, moving toward Story occasionally. With no sunlight it was obvious this wasn't a reflection. The temperature, almost stuffy in the room, dropped a bit, but this presence did not feel like a threat. There was something comforting in it. Maybe Mrs. Wolf was checking on Story.

Celine slipped in after we'd both fallen asleep, and she gave him a pill and some water. I was too exhausted to ask what it was. Her kid after all, not my decision.

The next morning when I got him dressed, Story was wiped out from the day before, dulled and sad, like someone had turned down the color on him. The blood from his forehead and nose had pooled under his eyes into purple crescents.

There was that sobbing again, coming from the hallway. Story's eyes slid over to the door. He had heard it. I said, "Who is that? What is that?"

He looked at me, his dull look punctuated by the purple under his eyes, and said, "Mrs. Wolf gets sad sometimes."

Call it sleep deprivation, or the harrowing night, but every single hair stood up on my arm and a lead weight pressed against my chest. I thought carefully and slowly and breathed in before I said, "And why is Mrs. Wolf sad?"

He whispered, "She's trapped. Like me."

That was harder to take than the ghost story. "How are you trapped, honey?"

Tears welled up in his eyes, and I saw this conversation spiraling and further draining a traumatized kid. I rubbed his arms and smiled, "Never mind, never mind. I heard Marcus in the kitchen. Let's see what he's cooking."

Story swallowed and nodded slowly. I had taken some psychology classes, but I was no shrink. It was my job just to get this kid through his days with the least trauma possible. His dad sewed stitches into his forehead with a sewing needle, and he was living with a ghost he imagined was trapped. A ghost who sobbed. And, frankly, I understood using that word in this lockdown. *Trapped.* We all were. This kid needed pancakes.

When we got into the kitchen, Marcus looked up with a bright smile that fell from his face the moment he saw the bandage.

"Oh, shit, what happened little man?" He caught himself. "Whoops, I did not just say that."

"Shit, Marcus my head hurts." There was that very Story twinkle in his eye. I was relieved, but all of this bothered me.

Marcus said, "I know, I know I messed up. But that's not your word. You know I'll catch it if your mom hears you use that word."

"I won't tell. I might tell Mrs. Wolf, but I won't tell Mom and Dad."

Marcus looked directly to me, the worried edge in his expression bordering on suspicion. "What happened?"

"He took a spill on a hike, pretty nasty, hit his head on a rock. Hard."

"Come here, kiddo." He crouched down in front of Story, searching his face for answers. "This what happened?"

Story rolled his eyes, "What'd the lady tell you?"

I laughed, so did Marcus. Then I stopped. Did Marcus think I was capable of hitting this child? He got to his feet and stepped too close for maskless comfort. I thought he was going to confront me when he said, "Is that what happened? Were you there? Did you see it?"

I guessed I wasn't the person he was worried about. "What did you think? I mean yes, I was there. But." I leaned in to ask very quietly, "Do they hit him?"

He nodded over to the breakfast nook, and I slid in opposite Story. He put some pancakes down in front of him.

Marcus said, "He's gonna need a tetanus shot."

Story said, "A SHOT?"

Marcus closed his eyes, clearly wishing he hadn't said it. "Did they give him one at emergency?"

I was ashamed to even say it. "We didn't go to emergency."

"What the everf…" he stopped himself and looked at Story.

I made my voice as calm as I could. Kids listen more for tone than content. "They were worried we'd be exposed."

Marcus raised his hands in the air, half shrug, half *what the fuck*? He looked at Story, then at me, then out the window. Then back at me, "I'm not here for the childcare part, but you know this kid needs a tetanus shot, right?"

Outdoors, lots of animals, dust, cut, yep. Pretty much. "Yes, of course."

He bit his lip. "I need this job, see? And it's…not my place? I'm the food guy."

"I'll tell them." Once I said this, his face relaxed and he smiled that cute smile that was looking less cute now. That smile was, *phew, not my problem.* Marcus, my only ally in this strange world was starting to look less like a friend right now.

He said, "Story, it's pizza night."

Story's jaw dropped and his face would have lit up, but the gray of his terrible night's sleep and whatever that pill was that Celine gave him wouldn't let the light in. "Really?"

Marcus said, "Can you guys be back from your hike a little early this evening? Like around five?"

"Sure."

"I'll get the dough rising and we'll make us some pizza."

I texted Celine. *Hey. I have a question, can we talk*? She replied: *coming*.

I didn't know exactly where to wait, so I moved to the bottom of the dark carved wooden stairs and tried to look distracted by my phone. I could tell by her footfalls she had just woken up or she was on something. I wasn't entirely sure this woman wasn't doing the quarantine baked…or worse.

She wouldn't meet my eyes and her expression was very much that of a teenager trying not to look stoned for their parents. She said, "What's up? How's Story?"

"He's good, he's in with Marcus." *How do I frame this?* "Um. So. Where we were walking, where Story fell. It was pretty dirty. Is he up to date on his tetanus shots?"

Irritation came into her eyes, followed by a question, followed by concern. "Can we do that without going to a doctor?" This is one mother I couldn't really get a handle on. I'd met detached moms before and overly concerned moms, but Celine was a whole different planet.

"Where is his doctor? I mean COVID is scary, but tetanus could like, kill him. And it wouldn't be a bad idea to get the kid a CT scan while we're at it." Concussions were sneaky, he needed to be looked at. "I'm happy to be the one to take him." Because I would risk my health and go into an unsafe place for some rich people who couldn't be bothered. *Fuck.*

She didn't answer. Like did this kid have a doctor? "I need to talk to James." Without another word she turned and started up the stairs, but she moved slowly, like she was tired.

Ugh, I should get details from JF about emergencies, this was nuts. I went back to the kitchen where Marcus was cracking jokes with Story. Story laughed shallowly, like he was doing it to appease the guy. How young these kids learn.

I said, "Story, let's take a break from hiking today, okay?"

"Oh, thank GOD." He threw his eyes heavenward like a tiny teenager.

I laughed and said, "I've got a really, really good book I want to read you." I knew this kid needed a nap, and this novel I was reading was light enough on sex and violence to read him a few chapters. Lots of thick descriptions. I figured it was good to stay close to home in case I had to run him to the doctor. Maybe we could do In n Out Drive through. I was actually missing takeout.

I didn't hear a peep from upstairs until we were all in the kitchen making pizza with Marcus.

Marcus said, "And what does Mommy want on her pizza?"

Story said, "What are you kidding? Mommy doesn't eat carbs, you know what that will do to her figure." Okay, after all this time, he's still cracking. The internal brain bleed I imagined receded into my mind with the monkey ghost and Mrs. Wolf. We were constantly readjusting and making peace with things in this shifting world.

Marcus threw me a deadpan look over Story's head which I didn't want to acknowledge so I feigned going to the fridge. Once I got there, I didn't know what to pretend I was doing until I saw some olives in the back and reached for them. It was a lot, absorbing this family, its dysfunction, which I didn't want to know all of. I wanted to do my job, stay with the kid, get through the quarantine, make my money, and get out. But this every day of it, this inescapability of their weirdness intensified everything.

The doorbell rang and I got up to go get it when I heard Celine's voice echo in the hall. "I've got it!"

"I'm so sleepy." Story laid his head on the table. And the brain bleed fear was back.

I heard the door slam and Celine came into the kitchen with a brown paper bag. I looked at Story and leaned down to make a funny face at him, as was always my tack when there was something going on I didn't want to see. I figured Celine had scored and I didn't want to know where she kept her drugs, because then I'd be tempted to look and see what they actually were. Story raised his head and put his chin on his hand looking at me, amusement creeping into his eyes. He was on the mend, he wasn't getting worse.

Then Celine was standing next to me and shoving the paper bag at me. "I need you to give Story a shot."

"A shot?" his voice squeaked, and alarm shuddered through his whole body. Kids' reactions were always primal.

She shoved the bag at me again in a way that would have me tell someone, not my employer, "back off bitch" but had me saying, "Um. What kind of shot?" I got to my feet so at least the power dynamic could change. I had a feeling Celine was always shoving shit at people. Coats, bags, Story's lunch. That's if he was ever going to go to school. *Ugh.* This pandemic.

I took the bag from her, because if she pushed it at me again, I'd have to smack the bag or her to the floor. "What now?"

"We got him a tetanus shot from our…" She stopped too long to be convincing, "Doctor."

Oh lord, fixing parking tickets was nothing on what these people could get. I bet if they got COVID they'd be the first to have a private room and a ventilator. I took the bag and opened it. Rich people don't die.

Inside the bag was a plastic wrapped hypodermic needle and a little bottle. The bottle was full of tetanus vaccine. I had no idea how many doses it was. But a piece of paper flashed pink inside. I reached in. It was a sticky note. In bad handwritten Sharpie it read: *.5ml per IM. Same after four weeks. 6 mos.*

"I don't give shots." It wasn't entirely true. I'd administered emergency epinephrine and had one kid with diabetes I had to give an insulin shot daily for a while there. But I had to draw a line somewhere. Celine needed pushback.

Celine let out an exasperated "ugh!" and stormed out of the room, her patchouli stinky feet smell going after her. Maybe it wasn't drugs. Maybe it was just depression.

Story said, "I'm gonna have to have a shot?"

There was the sound of distant arguing and JF saying, "All RIGHT, Jesus, take a chill fucking pill, will you?" JF stormed into the room in his underwear with an open robe billowing behind him like a cape, Celine following like the smug kid who tattled. He looked at me, left holding the paper bag, and I tried not to cower as he strode over to me in full papa bear mode.

Marcus moved swiftly away to pretend to be busy at the sink, and Story said, "Hey Daddy," cautiously gauging his mood. This definitely wasn't his first experience of Daddy losing his temper.

JF looked at me again, and he took a moment as if he were sorting through a filing cabinet of roles and choosing the one to play here. He chose his cute, plaintive face. He tilted his chin down, his eyes up and a wry smile came to play on his lips. It was simultaneously mesmerizing and sickening. And he was wearing entirely the wrong outfit for this tack. He needed a nubby sweater or a simple T shirt and jeans. He said, "Sol. Sol, Sol, Sol o'mine…"

I looked up at Celine, to see if she was irritated by her husband so obviously flirting with me, but she was watching like a spectator at a cooking contest. She only wanted to see if he won or not. My stomach flopped.

I said, "I don't give shots, it wasn't in the contract. He really should see a doctor, you know, get a CT scan. Concussions are really serious business…"

His hand went toward me and then… He. Was. Pushing. My. Hair. Out. Of. My. Face. *Oh for fuck's sake.* And smiling at me, like he had at Uma Thurman in that movie back when they were both in their twenties. Like he only had eyes for me. I pulled back a little and his hand fell to his side, but his face got closer to compensate. I gotta tell you his breath was not great, but that closeness had a weird pull to it. I lost track of what I was arguing here. There was a reason. I had to push back if for no other reason than not to disappear.

He said, "It's not that hard, right? I mean, you've had CPR, all that training."

"They don't train us to…"

He cupped my chin in his very warm, suddenly there again hand. I was nauseated and trapped. I stepped back suddenly and fell into the breakfast nook bench.

He said, "Just a shot in the arm."

I heard a snuffle behind me. Story was crying. I turned around and he crawled up into my lap, curling into as small a space as he could. This kid's bullshit detector was on high alert, and he knew that he was going to get the rotten end of the deal either way. He was looking at his Dad with fear. JF read this and dropped into a squat and put on his charming Dad smile. He kept this look handy in his pocket, it seemed. "You've got this, right, Sport?"

He looked over JF's shoulder at Celine, who pulled out her mom smile. She nodded at him.

Story said, "Only if Soley does it for me."

I was irritated and warmed by the new nickname. He scooted off my lap and pulled a footstool out of the island which he heaved himself up onto. And he pulled his sleeve up.

I said, "Okay, let me…" *Fuck. Fuck these people.*

JF said, "Great!" And like the wraiths they were, JF and Celine slunk out the door and disappeared back to their lair. Marcus made a disapproving noise like an old woman *Mmm-Mmm-Mmmm.* He opened the oven, sliding a baking tray in.

"Okay. Well." I didn't trust the Sharpie writer and double checked the dosage for a boy of Story's age and size. Sure enough it was .25ml. I sat in the breakfast nook where my shaking hands wouldn't drop the precious liquid.

I should just take this kid to emergency.

But he seemed to be doing better.

And it was just a shot.

That night when I put Story to bed, he hugged me an extra-long time and I had to finally pry myself from his grip. "Okay, kiddo, nighty night."

I texted Celine, "He's in bed."

Story said, "Sol, if the planet is spinning why don't we fly off into space and everywhere?"

The phone buzzed back. Two words. "Not tonight." *The fuck?* She had missed meals, but never bedtime.

"Sol?"

"Because it's spinning is exactly why we don't fly out into space."

"Why?" Why was the biggest question of age four.

I said, "Who do you think would know the answer to that?"

"Not Daddy."

I stifled a laugh. I wanted him to think about scientists. I said, "Who else?"

"Mrs. Wolf. She told me that Missy hates her because she imburnted on Mr. Wolf."

"Imburnted?"

"Im… When you see someone and you know they are yours. Like baby chicks."

This kid was killing me. I said, "Oh. Imprinted."

"I imbrinted on you."

It had been a long couple of days, and he was going to make me cry. I pet his hair down and said, "Scientists, buddy. They are good at explaining why we don't fly off into space. I'm gonna order us a few books, how about that?"

"About what?"

"About space. Now get some sleep. Your mom has a headache and won't be down." I was lying for this woman now.

He didn't hide his disappointment. "Okay. You can turn out the light."

I went to the door and switched off the light, turning back to look at him. His plastic planets were glowing on the ceiling and the gilded stars on his wall had been painted with some glow in the dark highlights. That gentle purple light appeared, hovering over the corner of his bed.

Fair enough, Mrs. Wolf. I see you.

With this family, I was glad she was there. I said, "Goodnight, Story. Goodnight, Mrs. Wolf."

Story said, "Goodnight, Sol. Goodnight, Mrs. Wolf."

I was paying too much attention to Story this time on our evening downhill hike. But it seemed like if he fell again, that would be it. You get this kind of PTSD after a car accident. It's hard to turn right again when that's what got you into an accident the last time. Every little skip or stumble had my stomach reeling. I had to get over myself. This kind of hypervigilance, checking on my parents, worrying about the mail they were getting without washing their hands, warning them to clean their groceries was one thing, but this tenuousness at work didn't help.

My focus on Story as he made his way around the curve of the road, past houses built into the hill, combined with my overall sense of worry is why I didn't notice her right away. Her voice was so thin I hardly registered her, "Hi." Until the second, "Um, hello."

"Story," I called, and he stopped. I stepped next to him instinctively. Across the road, not five feet from us was the woman from before, the blue-eyed woman who had called him a different name.

"Hi, can I help you?" Everything was muddied by masks, so I tried to project as best I could.

She stepped closer, but stopped at the prescribed six feet. At least she was being safe. She put her hands up plaintively.

"Hi, can you tell me the name of your kid?"

Oh, a reporter, they'd tried to keep him out of the press this long. I was not going to violate my NDA.

He said, "I'm Story." I put my hand on his shoulder to stop him talking but the kid was four. This could blow up five wrong ways.

She laughed a little. "Is that like, a name?"

Even under his mask he looked hurt, but she said, "I'm sorry, honey. Antonio. Don't you remember? Tonito." She wasn't determined, she was trying him out. It was the look on Story's face when he heard the name that surprised me. Was that recognition?

He murmured, "Tonitotito." There was a spell to that murmur, something sacred.

Tears sprang to the woman's eyes as if he'd flipped a switch. She said, "I knew it. Oh lord, I knew it. Oh, God, oh, God."

"Sol, I don't feel so good." I saw tears coming to his eyes, too. I crouched down and picked him up. The *Don't crouch*! command came through from my mountain lion training, but this was no mountain lion. My hypervigilance turned into a cyclone of uneasiness, all the wrong pistons firing. But the primary one firing now was *danger. Leave. Now.*

"Please," the woman said, "Can you take his mask down so I can see him? What happened to his head?" Tears were streaming down her face now. She was half excited, half frantic.

I said, "We've got to get home." There was a connection between these two. It felt weirdly wrong to keep them apart. I had to do my job. Maybe this was an adoption. Maybe she was breaking the terms of the contract. No one had ever told me the details on this kid. *The minute you laid eyes on him you knew he was yours. This will ruin us.* Snippets of overheard conversations spun through my head, but I couldn't land on any answers.

She would not stop talking and getting closer and closer to us. "Please. He…you work for someone don't you? I saw him before with someone else. Who is he living with?"

"I'm not at liberty to say." The entire summer, the place to stay, the threat they'd come after my family and sue me, that fifteen thousand dollars I was counting on, all of this was telling me *get away*. But still, there was something there.

"You misunderstand. This is Antonio. This is my *son*." Her voice was desperate, cracking.

Story's voice came out in panicked breaths. "Sol, home now. Home please. Home."

"He was taken from me. He was only eighteen months old. We were in a park." She was crazed but trying, so hard to appear calm. She danced on the balls of her feet and shook her hands out and said. "He was kidnapped." The panic thrumming around this woman who was working so hard to stay calm ended up feeling something like crazy to me. I backed away, Story behind me.

If I went straight back, she'd know, she'd follow. I fumbled for my phone and called Marcus. "Can you come get me? Dropping a pin. Emergency." I hung up and picked Story up. He wrapped his legs around me and lay his head on my shoulder, burying his face in my neck. I started walking further down the hill as quickly as I could given his weight. No way I was going to lead this woman to the house.

The woman hollered after me, "I've been looking for so long. I saw him when you were walking last time. I knew. You know when you *know?*" Her voice kept rising in tone, cracking, and the more she talked the more of a threat I felt. People always got weird around stars, stars' children. I remember this crazed classmate in high school saving up coins to call Brad Pitt's sister from a payphone. It always gets weird like that. "Antonio!" the voice was a garbled cry and Story clutched me tighter.

Story's response was the one that made me wonder. That Tonito thing. But I served this boy first and he said *home*. Marcus's car rounded the curve and skidded to a stop just near us. I ran to the passenger door to get in.

The woman ran up to the car and said, "Look up Dolores Winchell. Look up Antonio." *Dolores. Antonio.* The way she pronounced the names, however white presenting this woman was, she was clearly Latina. This stabbed me somewhere in the gut. I got in the back seat with Story and before I had a chance to properly buckle him in, I said to Marcus, "Take the long way home."

"What?"

"Let's go for a drive through Hollywood, we need to lose this lady." We needed distance between us and her. Story twisted his head around to watch her as we left.

Marcus said, "Who was that?"

"Just some crazy lady. You know how it is with stars' kids."

Marcus said, "I don't like leaving in the middle of cooking." He was testy and that pissed me off.

I said, "She wasn't safe, it was getting weird. It's not like there's anyone else I'm allowed to call."

"Why not Celine?"

I looked gave him an *are you kidding me?* Look in the mirror. He understood.

"What's a star?" Asked Story.

Marcus said quickly, "A burning ball of gas."

Story was rubbing around his forehead, which made me worry about infection. He said, "How do they have kids?"

I said, "Sometimes they call people stars."

"Who's a star?

"You are, kid, you're a superstar." I leaned over and kissed the top of his head, hoping to fend off the inevitable influx of the toxicity of TMZ, fame, everything that surrounded his parents. That said, I was a bit worried about his parents in the first place. We turned onto Franklin, and I was surprised to find it as empty as the last time I'd been there. Part of me expected to drive through some veil from our strange castle into the normal functioning world, where everything went on as usual. That I had somehow lost myself in that castle with the screeching monkey and its weeping ghosts. But the quarantine was still on everywhere, and people were scarce.

Later we rolled down Hollywood Blvd in quiet. A lot of store fronts had been boarded up in the Black Lives Matter protests, and the National Guard was still stationed on a few corners. The quiet after a movement I had missed in my job, in my fear of catching COVID by being packed in with people in protest. Another thing lost to this stupid lockdown. My activist self. I was really proud of her. *Trapped.*

Story broke the quiet, saying, "I know that lady." He was so matter of fact about it.

"How do you know her, honey?" Please God don't let what she said be true. How could it even?

"Mrs. Wolf told me about her…" He looked out the window and started to hum, having moved on. "There's garbage everywhere."

I said, "Yeah, not a lot of people out to clean it up these days."

"Because we have to stay safer at home."

"Right." Dating, hanging out with friends, real classes. There was so much I couldn't do but maybe there was something I could.

A few minutes later as we wound back up the hill, Marcus said, "We shouldn't bring this up with them."

"Why? That was creepy, they need to know."

"It'll freak them out."

He wasn't wrong, but it felt like my responsibility to let them know what was up. If Story told them what happened, and it looked like I was hiding something…

Marcus said, "Can I give you some advice, Sol?" I didn't like his dudesplain tone.

"I'm not stopping you." I kept an edge to my voice to let him know I wasn't cool with it.

"Don't ask too many questions. This is a sweet gig. I need this gig. We're being paid well, and jobs are scarce these days. Don't rock the boat."

Don't ask too many questions. Was this a mafia thing? Once Story went to bed, I was determined to look a little harder at what I'd been avoiding.

When we got back to the house, I agreed to Marcus slipping in the front door while Story and I went in the back like we always did when we walked. Of course, JF was there, sitting by the pool.

He got up as if we'd caught him at something and put on his pleasant, surprised voice. "You're back early."

"We wanted to help Marcus with dinner." I shrugged behind Story's head indicating it had been his decision.

JF bought it and said, "All right then. Go on in, I heard him working up something good in there." His voice was false, empty. His sitting outside, the absence of Celine, none of it made sense.

That night back in my room, I looked up Dolores, Antonio. An article from two years ago popped up immediately. There was a picture of a family, two older kids, a boy and a girl, around seven and five. Dolores looked young and happy, and with her smile she reminded me a lot of one of my cousins. She was married to a bristle-bearded white guy, looked like a good guy. The baby in the picture was circled. Inside was the story of a missing boy, but it was the baby, and judging from the inset he could have been a baby version of Story, but he could have as easily not been. When women lose children they see them everywhere, right?

I went through every available interview and piece of press on JF. Twenty years in the business, eighteen famous after his breakout role in *Brenda & Lily*, and it was a *lot*. I found the interview where he first met Celine. Eerily verbatim.

I searched again, even for local records of birth, those are with the city and can't be obscured. No births registered to JF or Celine.

Then I looked up more stories on Dolores and Antonio. They were at a park in Beverly Hills, he was playing, she turned her back for a minute. They presumed he was abducted. The search ended after two months.

Abjustin to being a mother.

Fuck. Fifteen thousand dollars. Well, I'd been paid three thousand. I wouldn't have made more elsewhere.

I looked up Dolores's number, but I went out for a walk without Story before I called her. I was surprised she answered the number she'd left in the paper three years ago. I suppose she never stopped waiting. We decided to meet the next afternoon at the Porto's in Glendale. They had outdoor seating and, if nothing else, it had been an age since I had a quince cheese roll and their dulce de leche latte.

Ever since the pushback about the tetanus vaccine, either Celine or JF were checking in on me all the time. I was happy we got the kid the shot, the whole night just sat uneasy with me. Everything about it sickened me, not getting the kid to a hospital, Celine slipping in with the pill in the night, the way she shoved that bag at me, the way JF felt like he was playing me, the ask itself which was not in the job description. Which really shouldn't be a thing. I had to do weird things all the time at the preschool, it was just the *push* of it, the expectation from them. It all felt smarmy. A line had been crossed, but in the light of day I couldn't really identify it. And now they hovered.

The next day when I was out back in the driveway, with Story pedaling around me on his tricycle, I looked up and Celine was at the window, watching me. Such a look on her face, hatred or depression? Who could tell?

I stepped outside Story's room for a moment, and I nearly ran full on into JF. He grabbed my arms to stop me, and I wound out of his grip quickly, smiling with a friendly, "Hi."

"Hi!" He said so smoothly, like he was thrilled to see me.

"Need something?" I slid past him sideways, so my back was more comfortably to the open hallway.

He stood for a moment knowing it made no sense that he was standing where he was and lied very badly for an Oscar winning actor. "Just wanted to say hey to the little guy."

A sad part of me hoped maybe the scare of Story's injury was making JF take an interest. But the moment he went into the room he made every excuse he could to leave. I knew while I had him here, I needed to lay the groundwork for my excursion. "So, while I have you…"

"Yes?"

"Is there any chance I could borrow the car for a spell? I have to pick up a prescription."

"Oh, we can have that delivered." It was already decided. Like that.

"No, really, it's a drive through window. No big deal. No contact with anyone. And honestly, it would do me some good to get out of the house." I mastered an expression of hopeful openness.

He stared at me a steady moment, trying to get some kind of read, maybe. I could see him choosing his approach. It was gross, seeing the gears turn like that. He grinned a sickly pleasant smile and said, "Of course. We can go a bit nuts cooped up here. Where is your pharmacy?"

Even if he did call to check up, it was at least the same part of town. "Glendale of course." Nowhere near this neighborhood. I'd park for the Great White Hut. There was a pharmacy right there, if for some reason they had GPS tracking on the car, I could explain that away.

Those frickin' blue eyes. Staring, weighing. Terrifying. I held my amicable natural eyes on his. Absurd staredown. I would not lose. I had to know. I said, "Is there anything else, or can I go back…" I nodded in the direction of Story's room.

"Of course. Of course." He held my gaze a moment too long and left.

That afternoon, I pulled out of the driveway and took a sharp left down the hill, hands on the wheel, marveling at how normal it felt to be driving a car again. Even down these perilously winding roads. Once I banged a right on Beachwood, I rolled down the windows and breathed deep. I didn't realize I'd been holding my breath since I got to the castle.

JF had offered to watch Story when I was gone. Had offered. To babysit his own son. Only maybe Story wasn't. This was all too headspinny. I had one mission today: to hear Dolores's story. I had tried to train myself not to think ahead this year, to the inevitable spike in the virus, to the potential for my parents to get sick, to the election. I just had to focus on the right now. And right now, I was going to get coffee. With a cover story because the maybes were terrifying.

Dolores looked so tiny standing outside the Porto's. She was bouncing on the balls of her feet again, crossing and uncrossing her arms. I realized it was a crazy place to meet, they'd likely been backed up in the quarantine. But the line for coffee was distanced and we kept our masks on. I got a dulce de leche latte, two quince cheese rolls, and a potato ball and the familiar smells made me feel human and home again. Just the sound of multiple voices talking at once were more anchoring than anything in the past month. Dolores's eyes shot around the room as we waited. Worried or crazed? Or just afraid of germs? Once we got our stuff, she nosed in the direction of the door and I followed her.

"Thank you. Thank you again for coming." She said this asking permission, begging me not to leave.

"I just want to know your story." I kept an edge to my voice I instantly felt terrible for when her eyes welled up and her eyebrows shot up with worry.

"Let's walk. I have a lot to tell you. I want you to understand. That's my kid you're watching."

"Why didn't you call the police?"

She looked at me quizzically and laughed, shaking her head. "You work for rich people, right?"

If only she knew. I just nodded.

She said, "We're not the sort of people the police are there to help."

We started down Brand Blvd., shockingly deserted, but still home. I looked nervously for touchstones, for my old favorite spots, praying they'd still be open. Not boarded up. Pho Hut, check. Carousel...check. Oh no, not sure about that tiny kabob place at the corner. But worse, everything Dolores said confirmed my worst fears.

"I can't believe it. Like, still." Dolores's voice was a bit husky. I wondered if she'd been crying before she got here. She said, "I was visiting a friend in the neighborhood, she wussed out of a hike so I decided to hike anyway. Then I saw him! That's some kind of fate that brought me there. I never go to Beachwood."

I said, "Yeah, crazy."

She said, "Can you tell me who you work for?"

NDA, sticky area, but bigger crime here maybe. I decided a picture of Celine would be the best route. I had gotten it off the web earlier, saved it to my photos. *Showing a photo isn't the same. It isn't telling anything.* I picked one that wasn't on a red carpet.

"Oh my God." She grabbed my arm and stopped there on the street. I pulled her sideways to avoid the maskhole walking toward us taking up the whole sidewalk panting as he made his way somewhere like there wasn't a pandemic.

"You know her?" I asked.

"This. Oh my God."

Tears sprang to her eyes. "I wondered. I kind of thought," and then she started on her story. We sat on a park bench out front of BJ's. That was a place I wouldn't mind closing. There was very little foot traffic, so it felt safe enough. Dolores didn't know who Celine was married to, she just knew that face.

They'd had a conversation at that park in Beverly Hills. Dolores worked nearby and she'd always play with Antonio until the last minute before she put him in daycare for the day. Celine and Dolores. She thought at first she was another mom, but then saw she didn't have a kid. She was blonde, pretty, friendly enough. She told Dolores how she hadn't been able to get pregnant. She'd been battling cysts her whole life and after three rounds of IVF with her husband, she had given up.

Dolores thought she was fine, and didn't think much of the conversation and left to go home for dinner.

But the next day Celine was there at the same park at the same time. She told Dolores her name was Heather. That second time Dolores felt a weirdness, a fixation from the woman. It was creepy and she decided to stop engaging with her.

She stopped seeing her at the park in the next few weeks and let her guard down. One Wednesday, they got to the park a little late. She sat down on a bench at the edge of the playground and Antonio ran under the play structure to play with the giant plastic abacus affixed to it. She looked over to talk to a friend but felt something creep up the back of her neck. She ran to the play structure, only four feet from her and called for Antonio. She crawled under the stairwell to go after him, but he was gone. There were two entrances to this area underneath the stairs. She figured someone had snatched him from the opposite side. She swears, to this day, and the tears fell a little more quickly as she said it, she swears she heard him crying from the parking lot above the playground. She ran up the stairs, but by the time she got there no one was there.

"I should have watched him more closely."

"You were right there."

"I should have."

They had raised the alarm right away, called the police, the moms at the playground were good that way. She described Heather to the officer but what, too skinny, well kept, blonde hair? These women were a dime a dozen on that side of town.

Her heart broke, but she told me she'd know, she'd know if her son were dead. I did not disbelieve her. I felt myself tearing up throughout her story.

And my heart broke for Antonio. How scared he must have been. How weird to go from a boisterous life full of cousins and birthday parties and holidays to that lonely and strange couple atop the hill. How his baby 18-month-old brain must have mourned, in its primal, terrified way. I told her then, who Celine's husband was. Antonio's... *kidnapper*.

She said, "Oh, God. That's something different. Oh shit, how even…" She fell silent for a few minutes.

I didn't have any ideas. The police. The army of staff JF had, his agents, his lawyers. This man had power and influence. This was a totally different thing.

Finally, Dolores dried her tears and cleared her throat. She said, "Please, do you have a picture? I knew, I knew when I saw him, just…"

Of course I did. I showed her a picture when I'd caught him looking up at me in the sunlight of his window seat. He was in sharp focus, beautifully lit, his blue eyes bright in the sunshine, a look of expectation on his face. She took the phone from me and zoomed into his eyes. "You see? That fleck of brown, right there. That's a family birthmark." His left eye did have a fleck of brown that I hadn't noticed before. She pointed to her own left eye. I didn't need that kind of proof, I knew I believed her from that second encounter on our walk, that look on Story's face. I was just flummoxed. *Why?* I mean Celine believed in fate and the stars and all this other bullshit new agey stuff appropriated from 52 different cultures. She believed I was sent to her. She believed she met James on a fated day, married him on another. But how in God's name do you believe that someone else's child is your own? And how do you convince your movie star husband that this is true?

We started to walk again, and we began to plan. My first impulse was to call the police, but Dolores pointed out that beyond our not being believed, they'd think she was a crazy lady targeting a star, it would put Antonio on the front pages of newspapers the rest of his life and on TMZ, on trial. She could take him back and sue them, paying for his college education. But every outcome she imagined had her teenaged Antonio on the front page of tabloids. She just wanted her kid back and she wanted to give him the best life she could.

This was her show. I'd find a way to help her.

As we walked in the cooling evening, we had gotten all the way to the empty Americana, its vacant trolley tracks and closed-up shops, before we planned out the details. We looped back across the street and up the other side when we pulled it all together. We exchanged numbers and I hustled back to the car. I'd make up a story about stopping at Porto's for a coffee…an hour-long line. Something to take back in. For chrissake, I had to go back in and pretend that none of this was true.

Everything had been strange this far, but was stranger still was going back into that compound. The moment the front gate opened, I saw JF standing there, looking at me accusingly, Story on his hip. I pulled the car into its spot, quickly shoved the clicker to the gate in my backpack and got out.

"I'm sorry, I stopped for…" I held up my Porto's cup.

JF said, "Story was asking where you'd gone. He was worried you weren't coming back." His accusing tone made him sound like a cranky six-year-old. It was gross.

Story looked at JF funny and said, "I knew Sol would come back, Daddy. Why did you say that?"

My favorite thing about preschoolers is their inability to deceive. That said, it might become problematic when we finally left this place. I'd have to play that kid carefully to get him home without his setting off an alarm.

I realized I didn't have a prescription bag, I hoped JF wouldn't frisk me. I said, "Ready for our afternoon walk, Story?" *Antonio.* I pushed that name out of my head. No room for confusion.

I felt JF watching me with that steady blue glare. After two years working in a preschool and after a lifetime with my kid sisters, I got good at not showing my emotions, as amped up or crazy as they might be. I looked him in the eyes with the most gratitude I could muster and said, "Thanks for giving me the space this afternoon." *Who's the actor now?*

JF's stare broke and he grinned. "Of course. We try to look after our people, you know."

Our people. Just as well I was getting out of here. I turned to Story, who was the only place I could focus now with any genuine cheer. "All right kiddo, you got your walking shoes on?"

"I got my marching shoes on!"

On our way out the gate I texted Dolores. *Tonight. I'll let you know when we're safe.*

I couldn't tell Story until bath time. I couldn't have him melting down before dinner. Another strange dinner with his dad, maybe Celine. Bath time I'd tell him. It's not like Celine had been down to say goodnight recently.

Sure, they could sue me, but then they'd have to somehow get past the complication of having a child whom they had not adopted or given birth to living with them for two years. I knew all the details. What's the worst they could do to me?

Story sat in the tub driving his rubber duck around with a motorboat noise. He reached up to the shelf behind him and grabbed a swag helicopter from one of JF's movies. It was remote control at one point but had broken long ago, so into the bath it went. He made a *chofchofchofchof* noise for the helicopter. LA kids were good at this noise, even in the Hollywood hills.

"So, Antonio?"

His head jerked back, and he looked at me, eyes wide. I spoke steadily and calmly, "You know how you saw that lady? You were so excited to see her? You kept thinking about her?"

"My real mother you mean."

How even? Is this something Mrs. Wolf told him or something he remembered?

"Yes. Dolores. She…" Try not to fuck the kid up about his abduction. "You ran away from her at a park. Then James and Celine took care of you. Right?"

During dinner I had consulted my psychology books and a few sites to help Antonio through this part. There'd be time for the kidnap story later.

I kept on, "Well, she's so happy she found you again. And she wants you to live with her again. To see your brother and your sister, and your cousins."

His eyes were wide as saucers, "Mrs. Wolf didn't tell me I had a brother and a sister." His voice squeaked with excitement at this. I had closed the door to his room and the bathroom, but I still didn't trust the vents.

"We're gonna whisper about this part, okay?"

Antonio looked at me as if to ask why but then looked up at a space behind my head. I knew who he was listening to. He whispered. "Okay, Sol."

"Thank you."

He whispered, "Won't Celine be sad?" the swiftness of his adjustment to her given name from "Mommy" was startling. Once again reality was shifting. Story was now Antonio. And to him, Mommy was Celine.

"Maybe, honey, but they couldn't keep you forever. Not after your real mom found you."

"Am I gonna say bye?"

"I tell you what. We'll write a note explaining. And you can say bye in the note."

I'd tuck it in with my real note. My note outlined the many reasons why they shouldn't go after him. I wrote about my package on hold to *People Magazine* complete with photos and the whole story written out. I thought of the headlines, "The story behind Story." It wrote itself.

I hoped we'd be long gone by the time they found either note.

Antonio's helicopter spun lazy circles around the duck, *chofchofchofchof,* and we talked about what came next. What he'd most like to pack. How I'd come get him. When I was done, he said, "Don't worry, Mrs. Wolf is going to help."

"Oh. That's nice of Mrs. Wolf."

"She says she's been trapped so long it'll make her feel good *someone* can go."

I was done asking this place questions. We'd do what we did.

I waited until their lights went out. JF was very big on beauty sleep, and Celine was quite simply out of it. I packed the important stuff in a backpack, and took my body bag of clothing which I carried out toward the front gate. There was this hole at the corner where the stone wall met the iron fencing that wouldn't be enough for a person to get through, but it was enough for a bag to squish through. I heard it plop and roll a bit when it hit the ground beneath. I had spied it on our walks and knew a giant agave bush would hide it and prevent its rolling onto the public path. I'd come back for it another day.

I put my laptop in my backpack...laptops aren't cheap, and I'd earned only three grand in my time here...along with a few books and things I couldn't live without. I needed it light enough for the hike. I turned and took one last moment to look at what was my cushy, gorgeous apartment with sunlight and my little deck overlooking the road. It was nice, but life locked up in the quarantine along with the rest of the world was just less...wrong.

I turned again, heading down the stairs and out the door. I crept across the pavement as quietly as I could...hiking shoes helped. I watched their window and listened for anything. I decided to sneak in through the living room door. It's not like they ever locked it. I pressed the handle down, in disbelief when I realized it wouldn't open. Plans don't go according to plan, I know this, but the fact that I was reeling from a locked door meant I'd better slow my roll. We had all night to get this done.

I went around to the door to the kitchen which gave. *Thank God.* Marcus likely left it open for a stealthy entrance in the morning to cook for them. Marcus. He couldn't be blamed for any of this. But without Story to cook for would they need him? They needed their shakes, I guess. I couldn't think about it. With tons of celebrities who can't cook Safer at Home, Marcus would likely find another comfy gig in a heartbeat and at least he wouldn't be party to kidnapping. I'd call him in a few days when it was all over.

I skirted around the island and the banana tree, hyperaware of my oversized backpack. This had to go smoothly not just for me, but for Story. Antonio. He could be Antonio now.

There was a familiar, nail-biting screech. That goddamn gibbon had... what, followed me here? JF had said he didn't ever hear it, but I heard it plain as day. *Mrs. Wolf will help us* felt like an empty promise. I wonder if she and the gibbon were at odds. Maybe it had formed an attachment to me and didn't want me to go. The ghost of a monkey lingering had to have some sort of twisted take on things.

I paused by the door to the front hall listening to any disturbance from upstairs. There was nothing. I stepped very carefully across the echoey front hall and into Antonio's room where I closed the door behind me. A light turned on suddenly and I gasped. There was Antonio, sitting perfectly upright in bed, fully dressed with his hiking boots on and a backpack sitting next to him. Mr. Bear's leg hung out of his backpack which had been zipped up in a hurry.

I whispered, "Hi!"

He smiled as if to comfort me and waved.

He said, "Hi. Sorry about Missy. She hates Mrs. Wolf."

"You'd said that."

"She's never gonna do what you want her too, that monkey."

Even ghost families were dysfunctional in this house. Time to go. I said, "Um. You ready?" I crept over to the shelf with the Oscar on it. I tucked our notes underneath it, hanging down enough to catch the light when daylight came. Maybe it was too heavy-handed a metaphor, that Oscar hanging in the balance, but it would get the point across.

Antonio said, "I been ready. We have to go now. Mrs. Wolf said it's time."

"I see you have Mr. Bear there. Is there anything else you really, really can't live without?"

He looked around the room, at his glowing planets, his custom bookshelf, his quilt, his desk, complete with computer, at his atomic clock ticking away. He shrugged. "I guess it's not really mine."

This kid was going to need a lot of therapy.

I said, "Are you sure?" *It's the least they could do for the guy.* I wondered if there was some kind of treasure to steal for him. But this wasn't that kind of story.

He said, "Can you tie my shoes? I want to learn to tie my shoes, Sol, but I think we have to go fast."

I knelt and tied quickly, double knots to be safe. I helped him on with his backpack and took his hand, smiling, trying to show all my strength and none of my fears. From the look on his face, I wasn't very convincing. I said, "You ready?"

He nodded. I put my finger to my lips and opened the door. We waited a moment listening. Story was mouth breathing, so, so loud. I knew he was terrified, his eyes were wide and worried. The idea of this little guy being so brave pricked my eyes with tears. We tiptoed across the hall and into the kitchen, but his backpack knocked a stool and there was a loud scuff. We froze for a minute, listening for upstairs.

I gently tried the doorknob to the back door when there was a huge gibbon screech again. There was a thump overhead of feet hitting the ground from the room above us and I pulled Antonio, who tripped. I caught him by the wrist and swung him on his feet again and we were off to the door out the kitchen. The front door would make our egress too easy for JF to get to. Action star training, after all.

A door swung open upstairs, its knob slamming the wall, and I heard JF's feet scrambling down the stairs with that terrifying swiftness I'd recognized from Story's injury. I knew he'd get to us faster than we could move, so as we went through the kitchen, I opened every cabinet in his path, including the trashcan one. I hadn't explained to Antonio how much JF and Celine wouldn't want it to happen, but he took a cue from me and helped. He pressed his favorite button in the kitchen and the Kitchen Aid bobbed out on its own little counter from inside the cabinet.

I grabbed the back door handle and turned, but it was stuck. I jammed my shoulder against it a few times as JF hit the kitchen. He cursed as he barked his shin on a cabinet, slammed into another, but the door was open, and we were running outside. Only by the enormous clang I heard as we hit the center of the driveway did I realize Antonio's booby-trapped Kitchen Aid is what got him.

"Story!" He froze in his tracks at Celine's reedy voice. She had somehow snaked through the mess and was at the back door.

No. Do I pick him up and he screams, making me the kidnapper? Do I stay and explain? I tugged his arm and he looked back up at me. He looked at Celine and JF who had skidded up behind her at the door, limping and bleeding from a gash in his forehead.

Story's voice was thin in the night air. He said, "I have to go live with my real mom now."

The noise that came out of Celine was somewhere between a plaintive cry and a wail as she sank to the steps outside the door. She said, "No. No, James stop them, you have to stop them."

I kept edging away, Antonio moving with me, and I said, "You have no legal standing here. Do the right thing and let us go."

James grabbed either side of the doorway and hoisted himself up and over his wife, suddenly in pursuit. He was limping badly, but getting closer when a flash of light shone so brightly it plunged everything beyond its reach into blackness. JF stopped, recoiling. "What the fuck?"

Antonio whispered, "Mrs. Wolf. Look away. Let's go."

We ran. I clicked the gate with the clicker I'd swiped from JF's car that afternoon. We slipped out the moment it had rolled wide enough to allow us through, and I clicked it shut again. Story said, "Thank you Mrs. Wolf." His voice, the recognition in it, and the warm light playing through the bushes surrounding the house brought a lump to my throat. How long had she been trapped there? Would this help?

We were supposed to meet Dolores at the gate to Hollywoodland. She'd have a car waiting. I didn't want to risk her being stopped by JF. I knew going directly there along the road was too obvious. JF would get his car and follow. Any neighbor, when presented with a white movie star, a brown nanny (the words au pair would not come up), and a kid in tow was going to side with the movie star. We needed to disappear quietly.

I said, "Morning walk." Antonio looked up at me and nodded. We started down the path toward the lake. I'd call a Lyft once we got to the point where the path dumped out on Mulholland Highway. The night was clear, and a wind was blowing. It was too early for Santa Anas, but sometimes the offshore wind had to remind you it was there. The smell of fennel and baked leaves and dust made my feet feel solid on the ground. Antonio was falling into his hiking rhythm. His legs were short though, and I knew we weren't going fast enough. I looked up at the house and saw that all of the lights were on. I was banking on too much…that they'd think I'd taken the road. That they'd think I'd called a Lyft or had a friend pick me up. For their two years in this house, neither of them knew the trails, but this trail was like a main drag for hikers. With a half moon and my eyes adjusted, I felt like we were sitting ducks. Or very slowly walking ducks with short legs.

"All right Antonio, we need to go a little faster!" He took off at a gallop and this guy falling and hurting himself was not something I wanted to factor into this journey. Not after last time. I shout-whispered, "Faster slowly!"

He stopped so suddenly, I almost ran into him. He looked up at me. "What?"

"I don't want you falling again, so pay attention, just walk fast?"

"I want to see my mommy." His voice was perky, excited, and he was galloping again. At least this mom would take him to the emergency room. I just had to get him to her.

I caught up with him and held his hand. The path was wide enough I could let him lead but catch him if we fell. I knew this kid was too heavy to carry for any distance.

Did we have time? Maps had told me this walk would take ten minutes for an adult walking at a fair clip. I figured it would take us fifteen or twenty.

"Story! Wait!" JF's voice echoed off the path above us. I could tell by the way his voice wavered that he was running or attempting to. He didn't know this path, but this man ran ten miles a day on the treadmill and lifted weights. He could run as fast as a leopard according to one of his movies.

Antonio stopped. The commanding Dad voice was enough.

"Remember what we talked about. We have to keep going. Antonio." I said his name like it carried weight, I said it the way his mother had. "We have to get to your real mami."

He looked up at me, it was too dark to see his expression, but he peered around me and by the shaking of his hand I knew he was terrified.

I turned and blinked in the dark trying to see JF. He yelled from the area of the house. "Sol, you are going to be in a lot of trouble for this."

Celine's voice cut through the dark as she said, "Get the fucking gate to open for fuck's sake, how hard is that?" The closeness of her voice made me jumpy, but the lake, the cliffs and the path were deceptive. Yes, she was right above us, but we were seven minutes ahead of them. No question.

Missy's gibbon screech cut the air. What did that monkey have against us? Or Mrs. Wolf?

We kept walking. The moonlight helped with our descent. Antonio said, "Sol? Is my real mom gonna remember me?" he wasn't being loud, but I felt like counting chickens was a risk at this point.

I whispered, "Of course she will. Remember though? We're being quiet 'til we get to the bottom?" Somewhere above us I heard boots scrambling down the hill, loud thuds. They were going fast.

"All right kiddo, we gotta book it. Coyote time."

And he was off on his customary skip gallop. I shoutwhispered, "Carefully though." I tried my best to keep up. A stranger would be better than what was chasing us. A mountain lion would be better than what was chasing us.

There were fancy houses lit up across the way, but aside from distant helicopters buffered by the mountains and crickets, there was little noise. I heard Antonio grunt a bit too hard and I slowed only to find he'd fallen. He was holding his knee and whispering "Ow. Ow. Ow." God love this tiny kid and his enormous heart. He knew the stakes here.

But the booted galumphs above us were fast gaining. I said, "Can you walk?"

Antonio nodded and got to his feet, but it was clear in a few steps that our progress was going to be slowed mightily.

I looked to the edge of the path we were traversing, the only way down would get one of us badly injured. And I looked up. There was a bush blowing about three feet above us. I pointed to it and Antonio nodded.

I hoisted the kid up in an awkward scramble and stood on my tallest feet and he swayed dangerously in my arms. I kinda threw him against the hill and he landed with a grunt. "You got it?"

"Got it!" and he climbed up. I followed, my knee scraping against the rock wall of the path. We scrambled behind the thickest part of the bush, and he curled into my lap. The boots got to us so quickly I wondered if JF had seen us. We held our breath and listened. JF stopped with a scuff, breathing heavily. He looked around, but only down the path and away from us. This is the part of the movie where someone has to sneeze, or a rock falls, or something.

The pause was horribly terribly long, and we breathed steadily and slowly together. As fast as he had stopped, JF was off, scuffling past us. Which led to a quandary. One way up, one way down. And lord knows Celine was at the top of the hill. We had no choice but to move forward. But slow was best.

We waited until his footfalls fell out of range. I scrambled down to the path first and held my arms up for Antonio, who slid into them. I spoke very softly into his ear. "We go slow and super quiet now. Remember when we were trying to see the bunnies? Like that."

He nodded. He limped ahead of me, quiet and scared, but I had to admire his tenacity. He kept moving. At that age, my baby sister would have had a loud nervous breakdown by now.

The wind gusted so strong I took Antonio's shoulders and leaned us into the wall of the hill. I heard a "Goddamnit!" from somewhere beneath us. We waited a moment. Maybe he had hurt himself and we'd catch up too fast. I listened hard but the wind was doing its howl in the corners thing and I couldn't hear anything. Then it stopped entirely for a moment, and there, in the distance, I heard that scrambled boots noise making swift progress. He was going to the right! That was where we were supposed to meet Dolores, but the getting out was the most important now. I took us left, on a longer path toward the road. Once we got there, I was at a quandary. Going to the right would be several miles, then uphill and then down Lake Hollywood through neighborhoods to Barham. I likely wouldn't get signal until we got to the top of that hill and Dolores might just still be waiting for us at the other gate where she could run into JF.

If JF had gotten to that gate and not found me what would his next move be? Would he climb the mile to home or go down the hill and meet Celine by car? Would he stop and wait for us? I can't imagine he would when we likely had gone any number of ways or called a Lyft at that side.

There was no signal on this part of the hike. There was no point in trying to reach Dolores just yet, but I didn't want her meeting JF. Did he know what she'd look like? What would that meeting go like? My only comfort was that his phone wouldn't have signal either.

When we got to the road, I opted for a left. At least I knew Dolores would be at the end of it. I couldn't imagine JF would hang around too long as it was close to several homes.

We rounded the road, clinging to the mountainside. We got to the end of the road where it turns into a path. I hoped the city hadn't picked tonight of all nights to lock the gates. I thought of trying to scale that thing and how would I get Antonio over? They'd been a little less vigilant about them in the quarantine, or maybe they were understaffed. I hoped the same lack of attention that had the gates locked late some mornings meant there were some nights they weren't. I squinted in the dark as we approached the gates but couldn't tell. Story got there first, or his eyes were sharper, and he whispered. "It's open!"

We walked through. I pulled the gate to, hoping the illusion of being locked would discourage our pursuer, but he was nowhere in sight.

It was quiet and the smell of fennel and wild sage pricked my nose with a lovely coolness that rose from the shady patches that hadn't seen the hot of the day's sun. I took Story's hand, and we slowed our pace a bit, walking, listening. Crickets chirped against the helicopters circling Hollywood, louder now. We had about a mile to go, which is a long haul for Antonio. I imagined JF was playing through a few things in his head now. Who could he call to help him get back a son he actually kidnapped? I knew the answer and the scarier question: who would help this charismatic guy no matter the cost? How many people did not give a shit about the law or real people but would love to be on the good side of a major star?

"Sol?"

"Whispervoice, remember."

"*Sol*?"

"Yeah?"

"Mommy's gonna be so mad."

Just the way he said it let me know he wasn't talking about Dolores. "She's not your real mami though, Antonio."

"But she said I belonged to her."

Ugh, the emotional weight she laid on him, while paying him no attention. "I know, honey. But your real mama..." good God, how do I phrase this without fucking this kid up further? "Your real mami is going to want to see you all the time and do things with you and the best thing, you're going to have an abuelito and abuelita."

"What are those?"

"Your grandparents."

"Mama said my grandparents were dead."

"Yes, her parents. But these are…they will look like your real mother, and you've got cousins did you know that? And a brother and a sister who missed you terribly."

"Yes! I have a brother *and* a sister!" He remembered our talk the other day.

"Their names are Claudia and Ruben."

In awe he whispered, "Claudia. Ruben." He started skipping a bit, so I sped up with him. Maybe hope could carry us the rest of the way.

My only wish was that the gate at the Hollywood side was also unlocked. That was a tall one. I kept checking my phone for signal. I had a feeling in my stomach as we rounded the last bend. I'd made my screen as dim as it could go, but still, it was light in the dark. Bars. It hardly rang before she picked up.

"Dolores?"

"Where are you?"

"Gonna drop a pin. By the entrance to the reservoir by the dam."

"I know it, gonna take me fifteen to get there."

"We'll be there in ten." *I think. I don't fucking know.*

I really wish there were more protection than the two of us. But this was the only way.

When we finally reached the fence, yes, about ten minutes later, I saw a woman's figure standing there, a cut out shadow against the lights of the city beyond. We sped up a bit, I clutched Antonio's hand. I just didn't know. Just then my phone lit up. I'd put it in my pocket face out, so the light cast a disproportionately wide glow around me.

"Soledad, we have to talk," Celine's reedy voice cut the darkness and her use of my full name was measured, controlling. It was the first time she pronounced it correctly, which bristled me. She'd had that ability all along. Antonio clambered up into my arms. I let him. He clung tight to me, burying his face in my neck.

I said, "No we don't. This is what has to be, Celine."

"He can ruin you, you know."

"And risk this story getting out? Talk about ruination." Circumstances had made me bold.

She let out a growl of frustration with a bit of a scream at the end. The same noise she made when she couldn't open the jar of olives.

"Celine, you need to go home. If I don't get to her, she's instructed to call the police."

"The police? The fuck? Goddammit! You signed an NDA!"

"You kidnapped her child, Celine. You're very lucky this stops here. Imagine the press, the courts. The scandal."

We couldn't wait there all night, and I didn't want Dolores to meet this woman. I moved toward the fence.

"Now let us pass."

"I don't think you understand. This is my SON. He was meant to be my son, always. I knew this when I looked into his eyes on the playground. The universe brought him to me." Her voice had a creepy resonance of certainty, I'd only heard the night of that tetanus shot. There was a *click*.

Antonio recognized this voice on Celine; he knew it meant nothing good. He stopped in his tracks and gripped my hand. "Nononononono…"

I squeezed his hand firmly. I had this. "We have to go. We're meeting your mother." I whispered. "Be brave, I'll protect you."

He knew what it was before I did. He whispered, "She has a gun."

In one of those retroactive hearing moments, I realized the *click* I'd heard was a gun cocking.

I turned to face Antonio. "Can you be a brave big boy and wait here for me?"

"Okay." He did not sound sure and clung a moment, but then slid to the ground.

Whatever happened, I wanted him far from it. I put my hands up and walked toward her. "Celine, slow down there. Stop a moment."

"He is my child, get away from my child."

A voice came from behind her, "This is my kid, lady, back the fuck away, and don't do anything stupid." The voice was strong and fierce, so different from the Dolores I first met on the hill.

Celine froze a moment, turning her head, expecting to be met with another gun? Instead, she was met with a flashlight from a phone, aimed right at her face. The light had a purplish halo to it.

"Are you recording?" She sounded terrified.

"Straight to the cloud, sister. You need to give my kid back or I'm going to make the biggest stink you have ever seen. You know what it is to be canceled? You'll lose the castle that's for sure, and when everyone finds out that America's superhero is a kidnapper? Woody Allen's gonna look like a saint by the time we get through with you."

I wanted to applaud. This shy, timid and worried tiny woman was twice the size in mama bear mode. With Celine distracted, I walked toward her and got very, very close to that wavery gun. I said, "Drop it, Celine."

She welled up with tears and the gun fell to her side, still in her hands, but I think she got the picture. I motioned to Antonio who ran straight into his mother's arms. At least I thought so from the noises they made, a hug, a squeeze, I was too blinded by tears in the dark to see.

Full disclosure on the nondisclosure: everything in this story is true. The names have been changed to protect a pretty terrific kid who deserved better, but finally found home.

They must have gotten the note because I never heard from them again. My safe deposit box of evidence, testimony from Dolores along with her backup video, and likely a return of some common sense kept it so.

I went back to my one room apartment in Glendale but felt so much Safer at Home. I was back in quarantine with the rest of the world. Back to getting groceries for my parents. Back to fighting my mom off on the front lawn. I was so grateful to see her again, behind her mask, hair graying.

I'm in touch with Dolores and Antonio's doing okay, considering. She has a great child therapist. She's hoping Antonio will adjust to life at home, that this strange ordeal will be a distant memory. She hopes he'll never get curious and look up JF. I wonder if the guy would take his calls. He's likely too chickenshit.

Wolf's Lair sold the following year to anonymous again. I said a quiet prayer that the next owners would find a way to set Mrs. Wolf free. Or at least they brought her a kid to play with. A kid who belonged there. That castle could use some new good energy.

As for me, I coulda kissed the ground at the community college when live classes started up again. It was the following spring before the kids came back to daycare. Cute-ass little germ trucks. I waited until I was vaccinated to see my parents.

The following Christmas Celine and JF were on the cover of *Us* magazine, a picture of them at the Oscars ripped in half down the front. "Celine and JF split!" Of course, I bought a copy and dug into it on the spot. "Irreconcilable differences." Sadly, nothing juicy about an affair. A quote from JF written very nicely for him, "Sometimes it's just best for all involved to move on. I loved Celine, love her still, and wish her the best in her life." Celine, it seemed was starting a wellness app. As my mom stood over dinner that night, stirring her killer pozole she said, "A wellness, app! Tell me more!"

"It's probably about how not to eat anything."

"Oooh, Soledad, don't be mean." She only used my whole name when she was scolding me.

"Stars are as stars do."

"Did you see? They just sold Wolf's Lair." Her gossipy tone had fallen away into a knowing *you are so busted* mom tone.

Oh, shit.

There was a deadly silence. I didn't know quite where to go from here. "I signed an NDA Ma."

She turned to me, eyes lit up, "I *knew* it! So, tell me what were they like? Oh my god, why did they fire you?" then, accusingly, "What did you do???"

"Mami, my NDA means if I say *anything* about my time with them in the next twenty years, they could sue me for two hundred thousand dollars."

"Oh." She did not care. "But what happened?"

"All you need to know is I did the right thing, Ma. I did the *right* thing."

She looked over at me, scandal left her eyes and she smiled nodding. "Of course you did. I raised you right, mija. Now set the table and wash the cilantro and cut the limes."

She went back to cooking, just like that. I was glad she didn't see the fact that I was tearing up.

We spent so much time before this pandemic worrying about stuff that didn't matter. I hoped the world was now as full of gratitude as I was for the family I have still living, for a roof over my head, and for the doable tasks of setting the table, washing the cilantro, and cutting the limes

FAMILY
SOLSTICE

SUMMER

ONE

Summer is my favorite time. Everyone is driving up and down the east coast visiting, and our house is a must-see, must-stop, never ending cycle of barbecues, boiled corn, laughter, flashlight tag, lightning bugs, and mosquito bites. We live in a small city, Middletown, part way down the Connecticut River. Our City friends from Manhattan and Boston say they're visiting "the country" when they're with us. Our upstate New York and backwoods Pennsylvania or Massachusetts friend say they're visiting "civilization." I like that we live somewhere in between. Whatever they call it, everyone has a good time.

In summer, Mama says, "Open house, open hearts, open life." She is the opposite of winter Mama, with her moods and silences. In summertime, she is hilarious stories, raucous late nights, hugs and encouragement. She's always laden with groceries and stops at the farm stand so that when she gets home, she carries the smell of strawberries, raspberries, corn, peaches, and watermelon into the house with that sapling undertone of wooden crate. She is chopping, grinding, sizzling, cooking fresh things, her honey hair falling out of its ponytail, her peachy-amber tanned face flushed red. She is the hostess, the problem solver and the comforter. This time of year, I can almost forget about Winter Solstice.

Our friends the Campbells are here, Gretchen and Josh are piled in with me and Jeffrey on the string hammock in the back yard, looking up at the maple tree at its midsummer greenest green. A breeze blows and relieves the stickiness I'm starting to feel where my leg mushes against Gretchen. We don't mind 'cuz we're friends. Josh sits on the wooden bar at the top of the hammock cross legged. Jeffrey's the only sib I can hang with anymore since Martina got too snooty to play all of a sudden. Like Solstice made her too cool for us. Which is funny 'cuz Jeffrey's older. I miss Carl though, he was my favorite. He moved out five years ago when he was seventeen and doesn't even come home anymore.

Gretchen stretches her long pale leg across my lap. It's too hot, but I allow it. The more we can shift position on this hammock, the longer we can stay here. I don't want to move from this spot ever. Soon we'll be called in to wash up, set the table, and it will bring about a nice meal, but for now I want time to stop. Here: the rustling of the maple leaves overhead, the creak of the rope holding the hammock, Gretchen's scratchy-ass razor stubble leg stuck to mine, an aggravated mosquito bite surrounded by the dirt her fingers got there when she scratched it, Jeffrey leaning on me from the other side, but only his head and his shirt touch me because everyone knows sibling skin is gross. And Josh going on and on way too long about some stupid movie he saw I can't remember the title of.

"So then it pulls off her *head* and her face is all *aaaaaaah!* surprised and there is blood squirting, like, everywhere." This is extra ridiculous because he has a maple seed stuck to his nose, the green wing looking like a katydid landed on him and won't leave.

Jeffrey is turning that particular green when he doesn't like hearing about stuff. He can't stand violence and gore, which makes it hard for him to get along with boys. But Josh is stuck with him for the weekend. Unlike the jerks at school, Josh is cool with Jeffrey.

Gretchen and I both say, "Eeeew gross."

And she punches me. "Jinx."

"Seriously it was so cool. They musta used a *pump* or something." Josh is frowning over another seed he is trying to split with his thumbnail to expose its sticky inside to affix somewhere else on his face. This is what passes for activity in July.

Jeffrey says, "Dude, did you see *Corvette Summer?*"

But Josh isn't biting. "Wait. Did you see *The Texas Chainsaw Massacre?*" Josh sits up, shaking all of us, "That was *sick!* Talk about blood. And that chase? Leatherface is scary as fuck."

Jeffrey falls back on the hammock staring at the leaves above him. He'll just tune out and let Josh ramble. It's how he copes.

And Josh does ramble, "Imagine that sick ass family there that whole time. Slaughtering people for however long. And no one knew."

That does it. One more word and I hurl. I whack Gretchen's leg. "All right stickymissstuckle, let's go. This is gonna get gooey."

Jeffrey says, "'Cuz it wasn't bloody enough." He's stuck, though. Josh is on a jag.

Gretchen and I lean forward in unison, tipping the hammock which causes a "heeey" from Josh, but he continues on his grossfest as I feel around under the hammock with my foot to find my other sandal I've left there.

Gretchen and I get up at the same time and jump out of the way before the hammock swings back to hit us. I say, "Let's see what's cooking."

"Starving." She croaks. She's not wearing shoes. She doesn't have a dog at home, so she doesn't know. I tell her and tell her, but I know it takes a step into a fresh poo to really learn why sandals.

"Starving…" Gretchen repeats, more croaky.

"To death…" I croak back in an old schtick that takes us groaning up the back stairs like zombies, scratching at the screen door. I sidestep the stair eaten to pulp by carpenter ants, a forever battle of the family. Not the important one. A shiver of a memory of leafless branches, a gray, gray, winter darkened quiet house, and Mama's closed bedroom door wells up, so I stomp harder up the last stair to bring back summer.

Mama unlatches the kitchen door, hooked in place to keep our fat mutt Gainsly inside, and swings it wide with a squeak that pushes the feeling away.

Gretchen croaks, "Mrs. Massey, we need fooooooood."

Mama gives off waves of fresh basil and garlic as we pass.

I say, "Fettucine?" It's not, really. It's whatever noodles are in the house and she mixes garlic, oregano, and basil into sour cream and shaky cheese, but it's the best thing ever when you're thirteen and growing even though it's too hot out to want pasta.

Mama pecks my head so as not to touch me with her mucky hands. "Mmmhmmm. Can you girls wash your hands and set the table? It's almost lunch."

The bright sunlight from outside on my eyeballs makes the bright yellow kitchen spark dark with white spots for a moment. I wait for my eyes to adjust and see there's a salad of tomatoes and basil and olive oil on the table and what, soda? Orange soda! Mama only buys soda once in a great while. Mrs. Campbell looks tired and was clearly in the middle of telling Mama something serious. She stubs out her cigarettes and smiles at us.

"Gretch, you remember your sunscreen?"

"We were in the *shade*, Ma." She rolls her eyes and huffs into the bathroom.

Mama and I share a knowing smile, because no one in our house would talk back that way. Everything is a little tighter with our family. Closer? We aren't the type to fight or talk back because we have more important things to worry about.

I think about this as we gather at the long table on the sunporch for dinner, all nine of us. The Campbells and the Masseys mixed in. The corn is piled high, the fettucine is never ending, the table glows with the colors of bright orange and green plastic cups, red paper plates and Mama's giant oilcloth tablecloth in blue with pictures of lobsters all over it. We get real lobsters tomorrow night. Dad has opened all the windows, so it's as good as being outside, minus the mosquitoes.

Against one wall under the windows lies a very old chest Mama says came over on the boat with our family, almost four hundred years ago. On the opposite wall hangs a pub sign, big as a poster, with a ship painted in white on blue that reads Speedwell. Dad was so excited when he scored it at a roadside antique shop in Massachusetts. Our family traces back to the ship Speedwell which is a Big Thing because it predates the Mayflower by, like, twenty years. When he brought it home, Mama thought it was kind of funny because the sign itself is way more recent, eighteensomething, but it livens up the sunporch and the ship is pretty. Our house is filled with old treasures like this. When friends come over, I get puffed up with pride, showing them the Wangunk tribal wampum, beaded baskets, the crazy old wrought iron lock Dad keeps on the mantel attached to a length of chain. Artifacts. Our family. Going way back. Dad always says the Masseys built this country and reaping its benefits is our birthright.

Dad stands up and raises his glass of seltzer water with half a squeezed lime floating in it. He never touches alcohol. Except on Solstice.

He says, "May our prosperity continue, may our friends always surround us, and may our summer be never ending."

We raise our plastic cups in salute. I usually wish really hard for the last part to come true, but this is my year. My first year to battle. I'm worried and excited, but also terrified. After this year, I will know like Jeffrey knows, like Martina knows. I will no longer be the baby of the family. I'll be one of us.

I'm allowed days off training when we have company, so summer provides plenty of breaks. But I have to admit I'm a little relieved when, after lobster night, after a movie day because it was too hot to hang around the house, after staying up too late, sticky with marshmallows from the s'mores, and after sharing everything I know about boys with Gretchen and her with me, the Campbells finally leave. Only five months 'til Solstice. And it's my turn this year. My very first turn.

We can't train when people are here in summer because it's too hot in the attic and Mama said imagine them wondering what we were clomping around about up there anyway. We need the back yard in the evening when the air has started to cool. We aren't all training, that doesn't happen 'til fall, but I want to get ahead, and Martina has offered to work with me a little.

After Mama and Dad are in bed, I worry because Martina has started breathing a bit heavier. I can tell she's going to sleep.

"Martina." I whisper and poke her. I whisper yell, "Martina." But she groans and turns over.

"Nooo." It comes out as a moan.

"You promised!"

"We've got like *months.*"

"You promised." I slip on my shorts and walk over to her bed. I don't totally sit on her. I hover my butt against her shoulder and just press.

"Quit it."

I think she has a crush on Josh. I think she's realizing it's never going to be a thing. Because we are nowhere near our periods yet, and this is definitely a mood.

"It's my year."

She rolls over and sits up, way more awake than I thought she was. She looks at me, one eyebrow dangerously up and cautions, "Take the night off. Enjoy it. This is the last year…" she stops herself. "Just fucking enjoy it, okay? And let me sleep."

There's a finality in her answer I know I can't get past, so I open the door and slip out into the hallway, closing it behind me. Our bedroom door opens on a room we call an upstairs hall, but it's really the size of a living room, with a bannister at the center that wraps into the stairs going down. Mama and Dad's room, Jeffrey's room, and the guest room all open onto the upstairs hall, so you have to be extra quiet.

In the daytime, it's a warm, friendly space with colored sunlight filtering through the stained-glass window at the head of the stairs. At night, it's dark as crazy and the stairwell looks like a giant black mouth you have to walk down into, slowly and around. But this is my year. I've got to be braver than that. And I definitely can't be afraid of this completely harmless part of the house during this completely harmless time of year.

I grab the bannister and follow it down, stepping softly to avoid the squeak on the left at the top, the squeak in the middle halfway down.

This is such a big house, and we are lucky to have it. The youngest member of the family inherits it. Mama was the youngest, which is why we get to live here, and because I'm the youngest, the house will one day be mine.

The house was built in 1902, a big yellow clapboard "revival of Greek revival," Dad calls it. He can go on until your eyes glaze over about the columns (Doric) on the ornate front porch, the gabled attic, the broad lovely windows framed with black slatted wooden shutters. The windows on the first two floors are simple two-paned sashed wood for maximum light. In the attic, they are detailed with intricate panework. It's is only eighty years old, but the inheriting part about the land has been going on since our ancestors—Mama's ancestors—got here all those years ago, when the original house was just a shack on the top of a hill with a lot of land around it. The family sold the land off, but this little quarter acre of it, this house, and Winter Solstice are our birthright. I like how solid and comforting that sounds: birthright.

I creep through the dark front hall and down to the pantry, which is called the pantry even though it's a hallway. Everything in our house is named kind of wrong, our den is called the study, our attic is called the den, but it's part of what makes it special.

Gainsly sighs in his sleep. I hope he doesn't wake up and start to whine for me.

The kitchen is lit by the dim orange light on the stove and I open the back door, squeaking the back screen open slooowly so as to keep it quiet. I step out onto the porch and survey the back yard. It's one of those funny, overcast, orange-tinged nights where the light pollution means it's never really going to get that dark. It's cooler than my room, so that part is good, but I realize there is no way I'm going to find a stick in this light.

I sneak back in, trying like hell not to squeak, and find my way in the dark, down through the pantry, through the living room into the study, where I feel along the mantel carefully past Dad's prize ship model of the Admiral Colpoys—touch it and you're toast—to the right hand side of the fireplace and down. My hand hits the fireplace tools stand too quickly and there's a rattle. *Shit.* I stop for a second, listening in the dark. I hear nothing until the house sighs.

Our house breathes. You can't hear it in the summer, what with people coming and going and the din of the crickets outside. It's most obvious in winter, but in the summer, once in a while, when things get really quiet, you can tell it's still there.

I'll really freak myself out if I listen too closely. Before I can hear beyond the next inhale, I clamp the poker in my hand and hustle it out the back door. I need a flashlight, but it's up in my room and I don't want to wake everyone by going up there again, so I grab the heavy wooden pepper grinder from the kitchen table as a substitute. I take great care with the back door again and step out into the yard.

I follow the stepping stones carefully down to the part of the yard where Gainsly can't reach. I don't need to add dog shit to this exercise. Poker gripped in the right hand, pepper shaker in the left. The substitute flashlight isn't a big deal, I just need the weight for training, but having a real poker makes me feel more serious, braver.

It's two swishes to the left with the light, then stab right with the poker, advance.

Two swishes to the right with the poker, left with the light, advance.

Then three stabs straight forward with the poker and make sure not to look.

Don't look. No matter what you hear or think you see, do not look directly at it. This is very important.

A few rotations, steps forward and it's no longer cool outside, it's sweaty. I try to remind myself it will be cold when I do this for real. It's hard to even imagine in this balmy, mosquitoey air. Jeffrey says at Solstice, it gets so cold you don't even *want* to hold the poker. That you get so tired you don't think you can even swipe again. That's why the training. You have to be able to do this all night.

I practice until my right shoulder burns, until I am so sweaty, I start to stink, until the light pollution sky convinces me it must be dawn.

When I look at my clock radio when I go back to bed it reads only 2:30. How will I keep it up for a whole night? I have to train harder.

The summer is such a beautiful, lazy time and there are some afternoons you're so bored you don't know how you'll manage, or you read a book and go to sleep and wake up sweaty and slick because the afternoon has turned from hot to HOT. Or a thunderstorm comes, and you get so excited by the darkening sky and the rain, but it leaves it hotter than it was before. But the sneaky thing about summer is it seems forever and you can get into that dream state, but suddenly it's Labor Day weekend with the last round of guests and Mama makes one big last feast with marinated flank steak roasted on the barbecue, its edges crunchy where Dad let it slide into the charcoal just a little and the strawberry shortcake has turned to peach, but suddenly the sun porch starts to get chilly after dessert and you know school starts Tuesday and like that, it's all over.

FALL

TWO

First day of school, Martina's alarm goes off at the crack. I don't know what about hitting age fifteen has made her so damn high maintenance, but all of a sudden she needs an extra hour for blow drying, for makeup, for tinny music playing out of her Walkman, for laughs or irritated sighs. I think she was saving up all those late sleeping mornings in the summer to punish me now. It's hardly even light out and she's all over the room thunking, flopping, and worse, bitching at me. "How many times I gotta tell you, you can't go through my shit? Now I can't fucking find *anything*." And if it was one, two, even three noises, I could go back to sleep for a bit more. But she's on the side of my bed bouncing it and yelling in my ear, "Don't go through my *shiiiiit*." She prolongs the last syllable into a punishing yell so close to my ear that I feel her wet breath. Gross.

I muffle into my pillow, "Shut up, I couldn't find any navy socks and you don't even have to wear them anymore."

It's not like anything she does, hair, makeup, clothes can make her look any different. The Masseys all look the same. Honey to brown hair, flat blue eyes, bulgy noses that look cute when you're little, too big when you're a teenager. And the thing about Martina, she looks so much like Mama, it's creepy. Only a Mama with heavy blue eye shadow and super pink lipstick.

She lets out an exasperated *ugh* and mercifully leaves the room, closing the door. Now I can finally… Well, damn it. I'm awake anyway.

Mama really does for us on that first day of school. She has us get our stuff together the night before, makes us lunches, and for breakfast? Pancakes. You have to understand, we are a cereal and English muffin get your own kind of family. So homemade breakfast is a big deal.

Jeffrey looks a little peaky this morning, worried around the edges. He got beat up real bad last year at the high school. It's been going on ever since Carl left. Carl had only three years on Jeffrey, but he had more substance to him, more strength. With Carl, you knew you'd be taken care of, and the kids who knew him wouldn't mess with Jeffrey. I was sad when Carl left without even saying goodbye, but when Jeffrey came home in sixth grade with a black eye and a broken rib, it really pissed me off. Bailing on us like that, like we'd be fine without him. It's been like this for Jeffrey at school ever since.

Mama puts a heavy plate of pancakes on the table and things feel comfy and right, but she won't stop staring at me. When I catch her, she smiles, and looks away, or gets to some task or other. Syrup. Dishes. Lunches. Any time it gets quiet I find her flat, blue, Massey eyes resting on me once again. I don't remember her ever getting weird this early before. Usually she doesn't get fully weird 'til November. But maybe it's because it's my year. And maybe I didn't notice her looking at Martina that way two years ago, or Jeffrey three years ago. Maybe you only notice it when you're the one being looked at.

Every year around November, Mama changes completely, gets quiet, gets introspective, moody. And by December, she's not so much talking to us. But this is the first day of school, and there's usually a solid change in the weather before I can feel this from her. I feel it now, as she looks at me over her coffee, as she leans on the counter, as her first day of school smile doesn't seem to reach her eyes. And I get the sick dread that doesn't usually hit me until the bottom half of November, after the Halloween candy is gone. Because however bad Solstice is, Mama's change around that time of year is worse.

When Dad scoots by her sideways, leans in and kisses her, rubs her shoulders comfortingly, and puts his hand to the side of her face, I know something is up.

Martina and Jeffrey have a school bus, but Dad still has to drive me to school. He drops me before going to the office. Mama says he's a manager at the paper mill, but I'm not entirely sure what that means. The nice thing about Dad is that he isn't about his work as much as he's about his family. All I know is he's home every night around five, hanging out in his favorite spot, the comfy leather office chair at Grandpa's ancient wooden desk in the den. More "Massey treasure," as he calls it. We can be sure to find him there after work if we need help with homework, if we need quiet company, or life advice. I've learned from my friends that the dad who is always around is a rare thing.

When Mama and Dad got married, Dad took the Massey name. I thought it was a hippie thing or something, but later Mama told me it had to do with the house, the land. Dad said, "I married this house." He's really proud of the Massey family history and all of its treasures. The desk was "saved" from "the great fire of 1901," when the house before this one burned down. The family saved only a handful of the furniture, mostly art and other treasures, like that ship on the mantelpiece or the deed for the land that hangs proudly on the wall above it.

Of all of us, I'm the only one of the kids who looks like Dad, skinny head, long body, but I'm colored like Mama and my sibs and have that distinctive Massey nose. Dad is super pale, his nose is pointy and his eyes are a muddy brown.

I grab my lunch and newly minted backpack, put on my new shoes, and slide into the old Subaru that smells like sunburned Naugahyde. Dad starts up the engine and we're headed down the hill when he says, "So, how you feeling about seventh grade, Shea?"

I groan.

He knows better. He laughs. "Okay then. You know what your sister says."

"Sucks and then it's over." I wiggle my toes around in my new school shoes. Stupid regulation loafer things, but they're more comfortable than last year's pair. I went from kid sizes to grownup sizes in one summer flat. Grownups have it all, even more comfortable shoes.

"Right." He's drumming on the steering wheel, in a good mood this morning.

I'm not about to let that good mood sit. "Doesn't help much on the first day of a whole year of suck."

"A school year."

"Still."

Dad says, "In a few months, honey, all of these daily nuisances won't be as big a deal. I promise. You're part of something so much bigger." He reaches his hand out and grasps the back of my neck like he does when he's proud. I always thought it was like a mama dog grabbing her puppy by the scruff. "I'm so thrilled for you, Shea, and everything you'll be stepping into."

That's nice and all, but he's been saying this stuff for years now and it doesn't take away the fact that I'm headed into seventh grade, which is still gonna suck. Martina and Jeffrey didn't seem especially happier after they'd fought on Solstice, in fact Jeffrey went to his room and didn't come out for a week. I don't think it's the cure-all Dad makes it out to be.

The Subaru does a slight lift and leaves my stomach as it sinks down, going over a rise on the right side of High Street where it splits to go up a hill. The feeling is so familiar and yet we don't take this road much during the summer, so it brings school feelings back to me full force.

Martina says junior high kids don't stop being major assholes 'til eighth grade when they realize they're all leaving. My main torturers, Jimmy and Suzanne had whipped themselves into a frenzy by spring of sixth grade, making my every day a living hell. Right now, I'd give anything to be back at home, surrounded by family friends, up to my eyeballs in buttered corn.

Dad rubs the back of my head and drops his hand back to the steering wheel. We ride along for a moment under the green leaves, the gold light promising a change. Mama's breakfast weirdness comes back to me.

"Dad?"

"Mmm?

"Is Mama okay?"

"Yeah, why do you ask?" his response comes quickly, it feels like it's pre-written.

I look at him. I catch a flicker of worry cross his face and then he firms into a smile and raises his eyebrows at me Groucho Marx style, like we're having a totally different conversation.

I'm not about to drop it. "She seemed a little more November than September this morning."

He breathes in, weighing what he's about to say.

I hate that. I wish grownups would just say the thing.

"You're the baby, you know. The youngest. She might be thinking about that."

I'm not sure what I'm supposed to say back.

He says, "Same spot as last year for pickup?"

Mama's sentimental. So, I guess that's a thing. But the way Dad changes the subject so swiftly, I can't help but think there's something he's not telling me. In addition to the other things no one tells me. At least this is my last year of not knowing.

Before I have a chance to think about it, we pass the supermarket and the school looms on the hill. I'm not letting the dumbasses at school get to me this year. I have more important things to worry about.

Carl doesn't come home anymore. I was only eight when he bailed. I loved him and worshipped him and when his friends were over, I sat outside his door, listening, pining, wishing they'd let me in to listen to albums or laugh or smoke. They were so cool.

When Carl was home alone, he'd let me come in and lie on his floor and ask him questions. Sometimes he'd tickle me or show me something cool or tell me things about life. Sometimes he'd draw me a picture of anything I'd ask. Skeletons, trees, dragons. I can't remember any of the specifics now, but I do remember it was after Christmas. But more likely after Solstice that Carl started to change and didn't talk much and didn't have his friends over anymore. He was hardly here at all, and two nights after his high school graduation, he was gone, everything cleared out of his room.

No one could give me a real reason why. I cried and cried until finally Mama, tired of it all, said. "Honey, you grow up and move away. It's just what happens." She meant to say it kindly, but it came out more as a *shut up already*.

Later, when I asked Dad, he sighed long and hard and said, "Sometimes growing up hurts so bad you leave the place you did it." I didn't ask more because I knew Dad had left his own family. For *reasons*. The kind of reasons he didn't talk about and it felt like it would hurt to ask.

Every time we sat down to a meal, I thought of Carl and the mythical Toby and I don't even remember him at all. Toby was five years older than Carl, and whenever I asked where he was, Mama got super quiet and Dad gave answers like, "traveling the world," or, "I hear he's in grad school now." Toby became this free spirit who wrote postcards once in a while. Part of me wondered if they'd all made him up, if they were having one over on me.

When I was ten, I had an obsessive need to write letters to Toby and was going to ask Mama for his address and some stamps when Martina said, "God, don't you *get* it? We don't talk about Toby. You can talk about Carl, but we don't talk about Toby. Can't you see it hurts Mama?"

All I needed was to have the words said, then every time I looked at Mama, I saw this in her. When Toby came up after that by accident, Mama's face would crumple or she'd leave the room suddenly, or she'd get real quiet. One time at Thanksgiving, I said, "I always feel like there's someone missing at Thanksgiving," and Mama's mood went full December, and she went to bed for three days.

Dad got serious with me and said, "I want you never, ever to talk about Toby again, do you understand?"

That's when I began wondering if maybe Toby wasn't in grad school or traveling the world. If something worse happened, like drugs, or prison. Kathy diGirolamo's brother was a junkie now, hanging out on Main Street and her family kind of ignores him. I wonder if Toby is someone like that.

Toby's only presence in the house is in a family photo that hangs in the back hallway upstairs, the four kids with me in Mama's belly at the beach. He stands in the back with sandy blonde hair and chunky brown glasses like all the writers wore in that decade. A turtleneck that is likely an awful color and those stripey pants. So much is hair and glasses and squint that I can't really get a good sense of him. Does he have blue eyes like me or brown like Jeffrey's and Dad's? Was he funny like me, brave like Carl, or serious and wimpy like Jeffrey? Were he and Carl close? Were they living together somewhere now? These questions nag at me every so often. There's a part of me that wonders if, once I'm shown the other side of Solstice, I'll know the answers. But even Martina isn't telling.

Carl and Toby grew up and left. But I'm not going to grow up and leave. Because I'm the youngest, I get the house. I'll be in charge of carrying on with Solstice. Maybe then I can convince Carl to come home for holidays.

This coming Solstice is like a mysterious corner I'll turn. Laid out in front of me will be the rest of my life.

The Saturday after the first week of school, we help Dad take all the cushions off the patio furniture and move it all into the garage for winter. Martina sweeps the patio, which has only a few leaves, some spent matches, a stray sparkler, and a citronella candle that has pooled with rain so long it's likely unlightable, the detritus of a summer totally gone. But this year, my heart skips with the preparation. This year is my year to work with Dad, one on one.

It's not like I haven't trained before, but I've been the baby in training for so long, when the older kids were the special ones getting ready for their turn. Your first time comes when you turn thirteen. I honestly thought Mama was going to put it off was for another year because I'm a cusp baby. She kept me out of preschool an extra year because, being born in October, I was going to be the youngest in my class. She said I just wasn't ready. But here I am, training for Solstice before my thirteenth birthday.

It makes no sense to me how we were just out here for Labor Day and it was hot and mosquitoey. But now, at ten in the morning on the Saturday after, the light is a totally different golden, the sky a brilliant blue, and there's a slight chill in the air from the night before. The crickets have moved from a constant din to isolated chirping. In another month they won't be there at all.

Dad gives me his softer, hopeful look as I assume the stance. Is he being gentler with me? He always barked orders at Jeffrey when it came time for his solo training, made him cry a few times. Come to think of it, he barked at Martina too. She didn't cry, though. She's tough.

"All right?" He asks.

"Tell me." I say.

"Swipe twice left, stab once."

I do the moves before he can get them out in words. He raises his eyebrows, impressed. "You've been sneaking around on me, haven't you?"

I flush. "I didn't…it wasn't sneaking. It was preparing."

"Good girl."

My chest puffs with pride. Dad is hard won and when you win his approval, it's like being named captain of something, it's like being king of the afternoon.

He corrects my elbow position only once and has me take a swipe at him with a stick which he ducks.

"Does *it* duck?" I say.

This flusters him. "You have to. You know I can't. I'm just trying to make you ready for anything."

The not talking about anything before they send you down into the basement makes all of this so hard. I argue and argue that how am I supposed to know what I'm fighting unless I know what I'm fighting? My arguments are always met with a smartass comment from Martina or Jeffrey. That weighted,

"Oh you'll KNOW, you know," or, "None of us knew, why should we start telling you now?"

I never. Ever. Get a straight answer.

So to Dad I just say, "I know, no questions, only knowledge."

"Attagirl."

Okay.

We train a full half hour more than he thought we would. I get sweaty, he gets sweaty, we laugh. I look up only once to see Mama in the upstairs window looking down. She holds a cup of tea and is too far away for me to read her expression. Usually, this early in the season, she might call out something encouraging. But this time, she just raises her chin in greeting and disappears inside the house.

That night for dinner is hangaburgers on English muffins. They're medium rare and soak the muffin so it falls apart. They've never been so delicious before. I can't remember which kid started calling them hangaburgers, but it was the family word after that.

I ask for a second burger and actually get one. It's not so bad being golden this year.

Unprompted by anything, Dad watches me eat and says, "I'm not worried about this girl. Nope, not at all."

Martina and Jeffrey flash surprise and then glare at me jealously, somehow managing to maintain that look of *you don't even know.*

I'm finally, *finally* going to be on the other side of that look.

THREE

Martina's first Solstice battle made me so nervous I felt like I was going down there with her. She was up all night the night before and I thought I heard her crying. I said, "And you're gonna tell me, right?"

She whispered back a little too angrily, "I told you I would."

"I know, but Jeffrey never told us."

She said, "I think it's just rude keeping us from knowing what we're going into. I think it's better a person should be prepared." She reached across to my arm and squeezed saying, "I want better for you little sister." I didn't like how, even just eighteen months older, she was always so superior, but right then, it felt good to be taken care of.

Martina's Solstice dinner was early as usual. At noon, Mama came out of her room for the first time in a week and went about the business of making dinner. It was such a different thing than our other holidays: Fourth of July, her face glowed and laughed with summer, Halloween she beamed and flushed at her pumpkin carving party when we could invite all of our friends and there were stacks of popcorn balls, candy and "Monster Mash" playing over and over, Thanksgiving she was subdued but full of warmth, filling the table, giving lots of affirming hugs. Come December, we knew better than to talk to her too much.

At noon on Solstice, she started bustling around the kitchen, and it was the one time we were discouraged from helping. She made a pork roast and potatoes and a green salad. Our glasses were brimming with milk and that was the only night a small tumbler of whiskey sat at Mama and Dad's places at the table.

On Solstice when I was five, I was sent to bed early with a pile of books, ordered to use the attic bathroom and not to leave my room for *any, any reason.* At that age, I thought the whiskey was a special grownup treat. When I was big enough to sit Solstice, with Dad and whatever kids were left at the kitchen table, I understood the whiskey was more like medicine for the evening. Like the cocoa Mama made us before she went off to bed.

Solstice dinner was served at 4 pm, half an hour before sunset.

We ate quietly, and then Dad suited up Martina. The catcher's breastplate was a little big on her, so Mama pinned it up at the shoulders to close the gap near her clavicle. "We can't have any vulnerable parts out, that leaves her chest wide open."

Martina's eyes widened behind the mask in the first fear I'd seen her show outright. And when Dad got out the duct tape to fix the flashlight to her hand, she jerked with the pulling and there might have been tears in her eyes. I looked away so she wouldn't know I saw.

The second time he went down—you went into rotation if it wasn't your first year—Carl had a sense of seriousness and bravado about him. Jeffrey cried every time it was his turn and his first time, he whined like I hadn't heard since he was a kid. The first time was scary for anyone. This was something we understood.

Mama stirred hot chocolate on the stove while Dad lifted the 2x4 off the brackets where it hung blocking the basement door. He opened the door, releasing its musty, cool dirt odor. He was always very businesslike with whichever kid was going down there. Hands on the shoulders, pat on the back, no hugs. It was weird, 'cuz Dad was ordinarily a very huggy guy.

Martina's year, I scooted into my seat at the kitchen table early and clenched my eyes shut when she went down. I don't know why, but I couldn't watch her disappear on me. I stood and watched Carl, then watched Jeffrey when Dad had to give him a final shove through the door, but with Martina it was different. A sister thing? I looked up only when I heard Dad put the bar back in its brackets.

We spent the night at the table waiting and listening, at first as the furnace kicked in, fighting that cold, and later, to those horrible noises, the roars and growls and clanks coming up from below. I knew the training, I knew we were fighting something, and when Martina came up that next morning with the dawn, she would tell me. I would be prepared. I wouldn't have to be scared like her, or at least I would know what I was scared of.

Mama never could sit through it. Every time, she made us our cocoa, poured a little more whiskey into Dad's, served us, pecked us each on the head with a dead look in her eyes and went off to bed. She made sure to be up early the next morning, waiting for her child to reemerge. But the long night was too much for her.

This time when Mama went to bed, with Martina down in the maw of I don't know what, anger forked in my belly. Here we were, standing watch for her, worried about our sib and Dad was toughing it out watching over us. Why did Mama get to go to bed? Why did she get out of this shit? 'Cuz she got more depressed? How was that fair?

Dad was always looking after her. He was the protector. The knight in shining armor, I guess. I made up my mind then and there that when I grew up, whoever I married wasn't going to let me puss out of life things. We'd fight shit together.

I fell asleep somewhere around midnight, my face down on the table. I didn't even notice when Dad carried me to bed. I just know I woke up with the weird light on the ceiling the next morning and sat up suddenly in bed. Everything was bright and strange. It had *snowed*. I looked out the window, excited, and was about to call Martina's name when I remembered.

I looked over at her face bathed in that bright light and a bandage flashed white on her forehead. There she slept, next to me, her eyes working on her dreams, and like that, she knew.

The morning after Solstice, the family woke whenever they did. The darkest thing had lifted from the house and you could find people zonked out all over, sometimes in front of the television. It was quiet again, that increasing breathing before Solstice gave way to the simple quiet of the furnace kicking in every so often to keep us warm. There was leftover whatever in the fridge and whatever canned food or pasta in the cabinet. Mama got up somewhere after lunch and started puttering over the Christmas decorations, already moving on. It felt like the pressure released from a can of nuts, the *pfff*, and we all could breathe a little more and move around a little easier. And best of all, we got Mama back.

Whoever fought the night before got the first of everything; they were allowed to be king for a day. They had the pick of the TV channels, the pick of the treats in the cabinet, the best chair that sat right in front of the TV. This was done without discussion or argument.

Martina would *not* wake up. I snuck down and grabbed breakfast and went back to our room to stare at her, waiting. I pretended to read like five different books and stared at her some more. They say if you stare at a sleeping person, they'll eventually wake up.

On Christmas Day, I'd sometimes throw stuff at her because I wasn't allowed downstairs 'til she was up, but this was different.

Around noon Mama came up with a sandwich to check in on her. She brought the plate over to me with a warm smile, her eyes weary, but alive once again. She kissed me on the head and then stood over Martina a moment. She held her hand just over Martina's hair and pushed her bangs off her bandage. She put a glass of water and two aspirin next to her bed and then snuck out with a conspiratorial wink. I guess she thought I was just being a good sister, looking after Martina. She didn't know I was waiting to be told the secret. I had a twinge of guilt, but screw that lady who hadn't even sat up in the kitchen. What was it Mama was making us do every year?

The first time Mama told me about Solstice, I was five. I was curled up on her lap Christmas Eve watching the lights on the tree and squinting until they spun out starlike in my eyeballs. Bing Crosby was singing about a white Christmas but it was weirdly warm that year, so it didn't look like a white Christmas was going to happen. I'd been super disappointed about that the minute before, but something wasn't leaving me.

"Mama?"

"Mmm?" She had eggnog breath. It wasn't alcoholy eggnog, it was the kind without and she smelled sweet and comfy and I had one of those Mom moments where you wanted to cry just 'cuz you love her so much and the lights are so beautiful and Santa is coming. But soon it will be over, and you will miss it.

I said, "There was a lot of noise last night and Martina wasn't in her bed and the house was breathing big and I went to find you, Mama, but you were sleeping and Daddy wasn't with you and what was happening, Mama? What happens when the house gets like that? Why is it so *angry*?"

Bing Crosby made the bells ding, and Mama's whole body got unsoft for a minute, hard like a chair. Then she wrapped her arms around me super tight and kissed my hair, and she said, "Baby, it's time for you to join us in the family story. It's a rich piece of who we are, and there are parts you aren't going to understand, but that's okay. When you're ready to learn all the things, we'll tell you, okay?"

Her voice got all reverent like when she was telling me about our grandmother I never met or when she was reading *Arabian Nights*. This was important. And with her tight squeeze around me, the lights glowing, and "Holly Jolly Christmas" starting, I felt safe and warm when she told me about Solstice. She told me how this was a very special part of our family ever since we first came to this undiscovered land almost three hundred years ago. How we claimed the land and built this country into greatness. How we are so grateful for this house and all it gives us, the warmth, the friends, the maple tree out back, the bounty it brings forth every year, so we can live and have these beautiful Christmases and grow all big and strong. But we had to do something for the house every year. A big, brave thing I would understand when I was older, and I would become part of that grownup thing that my siblings were doing for us. She told me how our family had been in charge of this very important thing, this safeguarding, for all our people for a very long time. But this year, because I knew, this was a very special year, because I'd get to start training with the big kids.

She bundled me closer, squeezing my legs around me and holding my whole body in a comfy ball saying, "You, my little bug, you are the most special because you are the youngest. One day, when you are grown like Mama, you're going to have a very special thing to do for the house." She kissed my head and whispered into my ear the thing she whispered into each of our ears when she got us alone, "I love you most." But there was something about how she said it that made me think that maybe, just maybe, she did.

That fall I got my first stick.

Martina finally woke up sometime after two. She blinked at the light, squinting and sat up slowly with a sharp grunt because she was sore. I didn't say anything. You had to let just-woken Martina get her bearings, or she'd hit you.

She drank the whole glass of water down and put it on the table. Her hand flew up to her bandage and she touched it and winced. She swung her feet onto the floor and got up.

"Martina."

She held her hand up, "one minute," and padded into the hall. I heard the bathroom door slam and waited for the flush. After the flush, I waited as she walked back toward the bedroom, but stopped just outside the door. Looking at the snow? Would she go downstairs? Was she gonna faint?

She came back into the room and her chin was set. I didn't want to believe her expression, but her words confirmed it. "I'm not. Saying. Anything."

"You promised." It came out more whiny than I wanted but *come on.*

"I shouldn't have promised. You just gotta wait."

"I *can't* wait. What about everything we talked about. Isn't it better to know? Wouldn't it be better to know?"

She sat down on the bed, pulled her knees into her chest and buried her face in them. I pushed the plate with the aspirin on it toward her. She looked up at me, super serious and said in that damned *knowing* voice. "Trust me, kid." *Kid?* We were only one year apart in school. "It's better *not to know.*"

With that, she flopped down in her bed and pulled her quilt over her. And I was left the odd man out for two more years.

FOUR

Halloween is two weeks after my thirteenth birthday. Dad is grinning and keeps saying, "Nope, nothing to worry about with this one. She's strong." To the point where it starts getting on everyone's nerves.

I have him alone one night on our way to Pizza Palace to pick up our weekly order of one garbage pizza, two pepperoni pizzas, and one plain. I say, "Um, Dad?"

"Yeah, kiddo?"

"I love that you have confidence in us and everything, but maybe, just can you um. Can you stop complimenting me so much on how I'm doing? It's really pissing off Martina."

He laughs for real and then turns nervous and he says, "Oh. Heh. Yeah, I didn't think about that. I'm just." He stops for a moment, "I'm just so proud of how you manned up to this, you know?"

"That's kinda sexist."

He laughs again, "Your mother's daughter. Okay, you grownupped up to this. Like, you're ready."

"Is it different from anyone else?" Seems to me Martina was pretty brave about things. Everyone who came before seems pretty brave to me.

"Are you kidding? Carl was totally terrified. He cried the night before Solstice. You don't remember?"

"I was like three, Dad."

"When it came time, he manned up, but whoah, he was pretty worked up leading up to it."

"Dad."

"Sorry. I know. I'm just saying. And Jeffrey." He rolls his eyes. He knows I know Jeffrey's a total wimp. I can still hear that last yelp as Dad shoved him through the door and barred it behind him.

Dad pulls into the parking lot and I smell that gorgeous pizza tinge to the air. My mouth starts watering. With all the training, I'm always hungry these days. He says, "You're a good kid, Shea. Don't let anyone tell you different.

You're a solid…" I can tell he's rewriting wherever his fifties brain has gone. "You are an excellent human being."

"We'll make a feminist of you yet, Dad."

On the way home, the pizzas, so toasty and delicious smelling, weigh my lap down, making my thighs sweat through my jeans. It's a singular feeling, the cold night, the warm pizzas, the smell filling the car. A whole different animal in the spring. I have to ask. "And Toby?"

"What?" He didn't hear it and then he does hear it and reprimands. "Shea."

"Was Toby brave?"

"Shea, what have I told you."

"Dad."

He doesn't answer and we drive another half a mile before he says, "Toby was the bravest of all. But you are not to mention him ever, especially in front of Mama, okay?"

"Okay." This doesn't jive with my idea of Toby burnt out somewhere in a different town. I say, "Does Toby…"

He cuts me off in a terrifying voice I rarely hear him use, he says, "Do you understand me?"

"Yes, sir."

I sit back, no longer hungry, ashamed that I even brought it up.

When I was very small, it was the third rainy afternoon in a row one summer and I snuck up to the attic where I heard Carl, Jeffrey and Martina playing. I wasn't allowed up there because there were roofing nails sticking out of the wood and lathe ceiling and Mama worried I'd bonk my head and get tetanus, but what was I supposed to do for three days alone in my room? I stood on the third step down looking through the railing, the floor of the attic level with my nose. The attic was bare warm colored wood, floor and slanted ceilings done in wide planks. It had windows all around, and was usually bright, but today was the kind of gray that made everything dingy.

In the corner on the right was a fort made of cardboard boxes full of stuff. Carl had pulled an electric lamp in there and run the cord into Toby's room. Toby's room was just off the attic and had the coveted clawfoot tub. Now that he was gone, no one was allowed in there. But I was the age when I started to notice that the older kids didn't always do what they were supposed to.

Martina had a strain in her voice when she said, "It's too tight." Her voice came from the other side of the attic, so I slid silently across the stair and peeked out through the other railing. The rain was extra loud, fat, steady pattering on the uninsulated roof.

Carl said, "You're there forever, it's gotta be tight."

Martina said, "I don't like this game."

Jeffrey said, "It's a very important game and even if Carl won't tell us why, I think we have to do it."

Martina was tied to the chimney, which rose up through the center of the house from the front hall. She looked so weird in her aqua shorts and stripey T-shirt, her hair still bed mussy, cords tied around her. She squirmed to get free.

Carl stood over her, hands on his hips. He said, "Martina, it is your duty to protect us all. And to protect us all you must be bound." He sounded somber, important.

Martina said, "It's hard to breathe. Jeffrey get me out of here."

He said, "We get the point, Carl. What's the next part?"

Carl said, "We have to be strong. We have to know this, and we have to leave her."

"You're not gonna. No, Carl, c'mon." There was an edge of tears in her voice.

"It's not funny, Carl, let her go." Jeffrey had tears in his voice, too. I didn't know why my favorite brother was making everyone so miserable.

Carl started walking toward the stairs and I gasped and stepped down a step, ducking below the edge of the floor.

Martina said, "I'm going to tell Mama."

"Mama knows. Everyone knows." His voice was heavy and horrible.

Jeffrey said, "Shut up. You're a total creep." He leaned in and started untying Martina.

Carl said, "Fine. But you don't know. You don't *know*." He stormed right past the staircase into Toby's room and slammed the door.

Martina was crying. "He's just so *mean*. He's never been downright *mean* before."

Jeffrey cleared his throat and said, "Let's go get some ice cream."

"Promise me you won't get that mean when it's your turn." Her arms were free, and she pulled her knees up to her chest.

"I think Dad got rocky road."

"Promise me, Jeffrey."

In a very unJeffreylike move he pulled Martina in for a hug. In a very unMartinalike move, she let him. Jeffrey said, "Promise."

I skibbled down the stairs as quickly and quietly as I could before they could catch me. I don't remember if I made anything of it at the time, I just remember thinking the older kids were weird and I didn't like Carl so much that day.

I put this away in that file of weird family moments when the olders were discussing things. But for some reason, talking about Toby with Dad brought it back. It was a piece of Solstice I couldn't make fit.

Thanksgiving we sometimes have the Mullins over, but they took this year to go on a trip to Italy. Who even does that? So it's just the five of us which means it's a little harder to ignore Carl being gone, the impending winter, the loss of Mama, which is so hard every year, and the overall pall, the threat that comes over the house. Mama goes through the motions and makes us roast duck stuffed with wild rice and with orange sauce and three kinds of pie which comes out to more than half a pie a person, but when you're eating lemon fluff pie made of frozen cream and pecan pie and pumpkin, you don't so much care that it's too much food, especially when there isn't a whole lotta conversation at the table.

Mama says Grace, and it's familiar, thanking God for all our blessings and allowing us to live here and allowing us the goodness of the house and I think she'll get straight to, "Thanks for Solstice and all the bounty it yields," but she chokes up this time and looks right at me and says, "And thank you God for Solstice. We know that it's sometimes harder than we think we can manage, and sometimes we have to give more than we want to." *What does that even mean, am I going to lose a finger or something?* "But we understand its importance in the larger scheme of things, we understand why we do this, and we understand when sacrifices must be made. It is our birthright."

Sacrifices? Oh shit, is there a dying animal part of this? Am I gonna have to kill a goat? I shuffle through all the past Solstices with all my siblings in my head and the only one where there was any blood was when Carl came out of the basement with an enormous gash in his arm. I don't think he cut himself. Mama sewed it up and ordered antibiotics from her doctor cousin on the phone. She said we couldn't trust it to the hospital. It was weird at the time and I remember this because that year I read the Richard Scarry book about hospitals and what they're for and there were definitely stitches involved but there was Mama with the blue thread sewing up Carl's arm while Dad poured himself a second glass of whiskey.

All of this blows through my head as Mama stands, staring into space and we aren't sure if the toast is done and I say, "Mama?"

And she says, "I love you so much, Shea. We are two of a kind."

And she leaves it there.

The next morning, I get up before it's even light out and head to the attic with the poker and a flashlight. The windows are black and the single lightbulb in the ceiling casts an orange glow in the chilly uninsulated space, its corners black with shadows. I tell myself the dark and the cold is good for training, but I know the warm, wood dust smells of the attic are a far cry from the cold, musty cellar.

I swipe, swing, and thrust. I fight through the fatigue of turkey and pie in my muscles and forge on for two hours straight before Dad finds me and calls me down to breakfast.

WINTER

FIVE

The day before Solstice is a Monday and Mama lets me take off school. She makes Dad take me out to buy me a nice dress for Christmas day; I outgrew the one she got me in September on sale. I'm growing out of everything. My pants are all highwaters.

It's so weird, shopping with Dad. Mama usually does that with us. Shopping at all this close to Solstice is weird anyway. We just don't do that. I think maybe Mama's getting me out of the house so she and everyone else can like, I don't know, throw me a surprise party? Cook me a special homemade something 'cuz it's my year? There's never been anything like that in the past, but being thirteen means playing scenarios out in your head that can or can't happen in equal measure. It's no more weird that this occurs to me than my fantasizing about having a loft apartment in New York where I can have my friends over and have a real hanging chair like the ones at that rich person's house we visited five years ago—it's a white plastic pod that hangs from the ceiling by a rope and you can turn it around if you don't want to face the room.

Dad's at a loss on the *where* to shop, so I tell him to take me to the West Farms Mall. I don't really like dresses, but because New York has been my obsession this year, I decide I'll get a black velvet dress. I wish I had some boots to wear with it, but we only have snow boots and practical clothes in our family. A dress for Christmas day is as boutique as it gets.

The mall is full of people, noise, and blaring Christmas music which feels jarring after our quiet, sullen house. Everything is too much, the canned peppermint smell in the air, the department store perfume, the damp of winter coats, the overheated aisles filled with people sweating in their sweaters and scarves as they mash together. I feel exposed somehow. Dad lurking in the girls' department, his hands hanging helplessly at his sides doesn't help things. I work as quickly as I can, sliding the dresses on their plastic hangers along the rack, *snick, snick, snick*. I think we're both relieved when, mission accomplished, we head back to the car.

Dad takes me to Friendly's and we slide into a booth close enough to the front door that it's cool and I can leave my sweater on. He hasn't shaved in a few days and looks all kinds of worn out. The restaurant's quieter than the mall and the fried food smells get my stomach going. While I want a tuna melt, it's getting dark out and I'm suddenly anxious about getting home, so I order a strawberry Fribble and an order of fries.

Dad's doing that polite smile he usually saves for company and sits over his coffee, which feels more like a prop than something he actually wanted. After a spell of quiet, he says, "So, kiddo. How you feeling?"

And like that, the fact that Solstice is *tomorrow* comes flooding back to me with a stomach grip around my fries and shake. "I. I don't know."

He smiles. "I'm proud of you. You've been training hard. You're ready to step up and step in. We'll have so much to talk about come Wednesday."

"We can't talk about it now?" I said weakly.

He merely shoots me a look and goes on. "You'll be stepping into our centuries-old traditions and your proper place in the world. Are you ready for that? To be a real Massey?"

The half a shake left in the glass suddenly becomes an impossibility, so I bob my straw up and down in it without looking at him. *Does this mean I'm not a Massey yet? And you married in, are you a real Massey?* But I say, "I'm ready."

He says, "Attagirl."

On Solstice, I wake up before it's even light out. I curse myself. I have to make it through the whole night tonight, and I can't do that if I'm up this early.

I squeeze my eyes shut and try to get back to sleep when the wind kicks up, clattering the branches outside our window. I huff.

"Scared?" Martina's voice startles me out of the quiet dark.

"Terrified."

"Sucks."

This neither comforts nor confirms my feelings.

She sighs, saying, "Might as well get up. If you can catch a nap somewhere around two, it might set you up for the night. But no sense trying to sleep now."

"Tell me about your first time."

"No."

I laugh.

She does not.

I look up at the ceiling where a parallelogram of light shines orange from the streetlamp outside. As if I've commanded it by looking, it shifts and shines white as some headlights go past. It must be at least 5:30. It's a Tuesday. People will be going to work. People will be going to school. Our family always takes Solstice off, but the rest of the world will go on as usual. Nothing to see here. Nothing going on in the basement.

As if the house hears me, it sighs, a long, long exhale. My heart beats faster and anything I've imagined over the past eight years floods my brain— from technique to training, to imagining a giant hydra, a fiery dragon, an army of people, a blackness where I can't breathe. I dream up a sharp thing in the dark, like whatever got Carl that time.

Two left, stab right, slide forward. I clench my eyes shut and try to blow my breathing which has come out in a gasp.

Martina says quickly, "Nuclear annihilation tomorrow. Today I will..." she thinks a moment, "Buy all of the ice cream at the corner store and eat it one spoon at a time, but only if you get the chips."

It's a game we used to play. My heart swells for her bringing it up. But I can't get a sudden new image of a pack of rats in the basement out of my head. Rats with swords.

Martina says, "You go."

"Nuclear annihilation tomorrow. I will..." I can't even form a thought. Those rats are poking me.

"Food, crush, or revenge." Martina has a steadiness in her voice, a guidance I usually only hear from Mama.

"Okay, revenge."

"Ooooh." She turns sideways to face me, although her figure is still dark.

"I will tell everyone I saw Kristen and Jimmy making out behind the school last year."

"And? Like don't most people already know that?"

She's right, there's no adequate revenge for bullies.

I say, "I'll smack them both wicked hard and finally tell them what I think."

"Attagirl."

"You sound like Dad." I drop my voice like his, "Attagirl."

"Well, I will beat them up for you if you need it. Nuclear annihilation or not."

"Uh. Thanks?" This camaraderie from Martina is unfamiliar.

Martina flops back on her bed. "Nuclear annihilation tomorrow I will tell Scott Cassella I am madly in love with him and I'll make out with him."

"Eeewwww."

"I might even…"

"Don't say it. Don't say it!" I squeal. This whole boys thing is not cool or fun. I don't know why she's so obsessed.

She says it anyway, "…go all the way."

"Duuude, you're like fifteen!"

"Sixteen next year and I don't want to die having never done it."

"Ice cream over that, any day. Okay my turn. Nuclear annihilation tomorrow and I will…"

We keep on like this until it's light out, and we make our way downstairs. The house is breathing steadily, like it's gearing up, just for me. Does it do this every year? Was it always this intense? The thin, blue sunlight comes in through the windows, leaving branch shadows on the walls. I haven't been afraid of the house like this before. It's our refuge, our home, our center, our place to hide out, to eat well, to have friends. It protects us from thunderstorms and rain and sheltered so many friends that January of the ice storm when we were the only ones in town with heat. But today is Solstice. We owe it something.

The humans in the house are quiet, but each one of us thrums with a silent tension. Everyone is getting weird. Martina gives me a huge squeezy hug for no reason when we're at breakfast. Jeffrey tousles my hair every time he passes me until I tell him to cut it out. Dad keeps catching me and patting me on the back like I'm a dog who's done something good. I wish they'd stop. All the differences in this day charge through my nerves and ratchet things up.

No training today, I'll need all my strength for tonight. Today I get sole possession of the best TV chair and my choice of television but since it's a weekday, it's only *I Love Lucy* and *I Dream of Jeannie.* No Sunday movies or anything. I turn on the soaps after lunch because of the drama music and the serious conversations. It all becomes blurred as I fall asleep.

I wake to a loud commercial playing an electronic version of the Carol of the Bells and the most Solsticey feeling ever, because the house is filled with the smell of pork roast and potatoes with a hint of rosemary. I was dreaming a springtime dream, perhaps because someone has put a fuzzy blanket over me and Gainsly is asleep on my feet. I'm sweaty. But here I am, the sunlight already waning, it's getting time for dinner and it's my turn.

"Good morning, sleepyhead." Trust Dad to say the cliché dad thing. He's standing in the doorway and a part of me wonders if he hasn't been doing the stare at you until you wake up bit. "How you feeling?"

"Fine." Horrible. Terrified. Upset. Irritated that he's asking.

"Good, Good." Dad looks up to the frame on the wall, which holds a very old, yellowed document with writing scrawled on it. He taps the frame, "Do you know what this is?"

"The deed. Yes."

"There was no one to draw it up because there wasn't even a town here yet. Your twelve times great grandfather had to mail it to England to make it official."

"And the land was ours. I got it."

He chuckles. "Well, kiddo, when you're all grown up and this place is yours, you can bore your own kids with that story."

Birthright. A quick flicker of excitement penetrates my fear. I kick Gainsly off my legs and heave myself off the sofa.

Mama stares at me as she serves the meal. Usually she's kinda absent, going through the motions, but there's definitely something new at play in her eyes this year. She stares at me to the point where it's creepy. I look right at her and say, "What?" I guess I said it too harshly because tears come to her eyes. She gets up from the table, walks over to me and gives me a hug, a kiss on the head, and she's out the door without a word. That anger that I felt when she bailed on

Martina has turned to a feeling of complete betrayal and abandonment. She's leaving me to do this on my own. I swallow some tears I didn't expect.

Martina and Jeffrey look after her, stunned, without a word. Something is definitely off.

I have to ask Dad again, "Is there something you're not telling me? I mean aside from all the things you don't tell me?"

He picks up his whiskey and downs it in one gulp. He gets up and walks over to the cabinet above the stove where the whiskey bottle is stored and pours another. A tall one. The last time I saw him pour a second whiskey was after Carl came up with that cut. And that was like forever ago.

Jeffrey says, "Is Mama coming back? What about the cocoa?"

Martina scrambles and gets up, "I'll get it. Don't worry about Mama. She has a headache."

I say, "What are you not telling me?"

Jeffrey raises his eyebrows and shrugs. "Look, you'll know soon enough. Then we can talk."

Martina makes the cocoa and passes out three cups. Then she and Jeffrey start gearing me up and offering last minute advice.

As she pulls the breastplate over my head, Martina says, "Make sure to watch that left lunge, he…"

"*Martina*," Dad warns. He says to me. "The left is important, it's the one you don't see coming when you're fighting to the right. And whatever you do, don't look."

Jeffrey straps the shin guards on my legs. "Is this too tight?"

I push Dad, "I won't look, I mean, I know, I know. But what if I see something? I can't help my eyes."

Dad, who is shoring up the shoulders of my breastplate with safety pins stops suddenly and steps around in front of me so I can see him. His face is terrible, his voice is worse. "Shea, what have I taught you?"

I flush like I've been smacked. I look at the ground and murmur, "Watch your feet, remember the moves and you'll be okay."

"Right. If you remember everything we've taught you, you'll be fine."

The worry on his face totally freaks me out. "Daddy?"

He pulls me to him, and my breastplate hits him with a *thunk*. "I love you kiddo. You're brave. You got this." He murmurs this into my hair and his voice cracks which doesn't instill confidence, nor does the fact that I smell whiskey on him in a saturated way that lets me know he's been drinking it a while. This year, that drinking is heavy and it's about me. And he never hugged anyone else before they went down. It's off brand for prepping the kid for battle. My clattering heart jangles out to my limbs with a newfound panic. *Why is this all different?*

Martina and Jeffrey get the duct tape and fasten the flashlight to one of my hands, the crowbar to another. Even when I swear I will never drop my weapon, they insist this is the way things are done. I'm pushed and prodded and tightened. My chest hurts, and I want to cry but I just say, "Jeffrey, the right leg is too tight."

He kneels and adjusts it and then smacks my leg twice when he's done.

We walk around to the basement door together. I might just barf.

Dad lifts the 2 x 4 from across the door. They always said it was for burglars, but I know better. Dad turns on the light, a single bulb that hangs from the ceiling down below me.

I look back at my family. I swear Martina's gonna cry. Dad nods at me and I step down two stairs so they can close the door behind me. The door closes, leaving me in the breathing basement. The *kathunk* as they slide the bar back into place seals it. I am here. For the duration. They'll settle around the kitchen table drinking cocoa and tea until the night is done. Everything in me wishes I was on the other side of that door tonight.

This is my first time in the basement at night and my only time alone. It smells of dirt floor with an undertone of oily singed furnace. I've only ever been down here in the summer with Martina for tools, or, on the hottest days with Jeffrey, to sit on the cool stairs eating Doritos and drinking soda. No one ever comes down here at night and Dad puts that bar over the door each sunset to remind us.

I hate these stairs. They are wood, and have a railing, but there are no backs to their risers. It's only ever dark blackness at your feet with the unknown space behind. Anything could reach through and grab your ankles. I get a creepy feeling around my legs like a million cockroaches, but I stand still an extra moment. Normally I'd scramble down to the bottom, closer to the ground, safer. But tonight, the house is breathing heavily, and I'm inside that breath. A million cockroaches beat whatever's waiting for me down there in the dark.

The house sucks in a furnace-deep breath and there's a clank and it exhales a sigh. I know I have to get in position, ready to start, or it will get the advantage. I grip the poker in one hand, try not to sweat too much on the flashlight, and start down the stairs, unsteady as I haven't any hands to hold the rail. I go one step at a time, preschool style. I breathe, whispering, "Remember," into the empty space. *Scuff, step,* "Remember." *Scuff, step,* "Don't look."

When I get to the bottom, the earthen floor is so cold it stings. How can anything be so cold underground? It's like walking on an icy sidewalk in rubber rain boots. I turn around and walk into the pitch black of the back of the basement.

In summer I asked Dad why we couldn't have a light in the darkest part of the basement. He said we just couldn't. When I badgered Martina on the topic, she just shook her head and said, "Solstice."

The space feels, sounds? Smells? Bigger somehow. Bigger than the basement ever was. Cavernous.

I scuff my feet along the dirt floor and the furnace kicks in. There's a loud clatter to my left and I swerve and stab a bunch of paint cans on the shelves that run along the wall, turning the clatter into a deluge of metal and thuds. I move my feet quickly so they don't get crushed. My flashlight hit the cans in the first place, but the poker is what brought them down. Fortunately, most of the cans are only half full. One of them cracks open and an eggy vinegar spoiled paint odor insinuates itself through everything. I stand for a moment, heart pounding, wondering what my family upstairs has made of the noise.

I slow my breath and flash my flashlight forward, peering into the darkness.

The "don't look" has a lot of questions and answers and explanations. But long and short, I'm supposed to look to find my way, but not stare at what I might see.

I slide my feet along the ground again, just like I was taught. The dirt floor scuffs up its own smell, but something else replaces it. The basement smells are supplanted by a thick, ugly animal odor. This is a reptile smell, like the stink of the lizard tank my friend Kevin had...only if you took that stink to the tenth power. As swiftly as the odor changes, the floor does too, and my foot hits something solid, but fleshy. I whisk my flashlight down to reveal a frighteningly pale, fleshy mass with reptilian skin. Like a tentacle without suckers? Like a tree root, but soft. The skin is a muted whiteness with yellowing pinkish hues rippling through its surface. I nudge it with my foot again when a grumble wakes deep in the darkness and grows. My own gasp startles me, and I carefully pick my way over the...arm? Tentacle? Tree growth? I move my way in forward, sliding my feet. See, mystery solved. Now I know why we slide our feet. Why couldn't they just tell me, "You will encounter a fleshy sort of thing..." Why the big mystery? Why only the moves? Couldn't they have better prepared us?

The groan grows in volume and turns into a growl. I remember my sibs have all done this and everyone knows Jeffrey's a pussy. I trained for this. I squint into the darkness and flash the flashlight to the left twice, thrust the poker forward. I've got this.

Something red glows awake in the far back of the blackness. The furnace? I squint to see it, and just make something out when I'm hit from the left side by a massive force of cold pale flesh. *Watch out for your left side.* I stumble sideways and fall onto the same cold, hard but fleshy substance. I yelp and scramble to my feet stabbing the air in front of me with the poker. I hit soft flesh and there is a sudden roar of anger from the beast.

I swipe the flashlight to the right, three times as I was taught, and stab left with the poker. Hit flesh. The rhythm comes naturally, has been trained into me. But nothing can prepare me for stabbing something alive. Even if it isn't human. I yelp, but go back to counting.

One, two, stab, stab, advance. One, oh shit. Stab. Forgot two. Two.

Whump

Hit from the entirely opposite side with a thunk so hard I see stars, I go over again. The hit is concussive, and I wonder what could have possibly gotten Carl those years back when he needed stitches. Maybe I just haven't gotten to the sharp part yet.

The roaring is merely in reaction to the stabs that make contact, but the growl rises steadily to a level that hurts. A level that makes me think I am somehow in the beast now.

Swipe with the flashlight two times. Don't look. But the flashlight catches the hideous hugeness of a full wall of this beast. And there's something stuck in the back wall where the redness is coming from. Is that a piece of plastic stuck up there on the whitish walls?

Don't look. You have to promise me you will not look. I can see the anxiousness on Mama's face when she told me this. Her insistence.

I look at my feet and swish the flashlight two to the left, stab forward, advance.

Roar. Piercing shriek, breathing.

I wonder at hearing the living, close-up part of the distant noises I've heard only through the floor over the years. The cocoa, the kitchen table, the roars and clanks below, muffled, distant, but harrowing. Now here they are, live, real, inescapable. I'm a part of those noises now. Whatever this is.

The furnace switches on and glows from an entirely different space from where I thought it was. Off to the left. That means the red glow ahead of me is no furnace. I swallow.

Swipe two to the left, poke right, advance.

I'm supposed to stop advancing and reach my standoff soon. It has to be soon. As soon as my feet meet something higher than the floor. They said it would be solid. They said it would be cold. They never said it would be flesh. Once I can't slide past that place, I'm meant to stand. And not look. And to hold it back with the very moves with which I advanced on it. To hold it back until the dawn.

Swipe, swipe, poke, advance. I'm still advancing well past where our basement is supposed to end. Surely, I've walked the length of the front of the house, if not another entire block.

Two more cycles and I hit it. I nose my toe to the right, along the edge. To the left along the edge. It's impassable. It's not an arm, tentacle, whatever, it's the solid form of itself.

And then you stand. And you look at the floor. And you swipe and poke, at a steady rate of one cycle every two minutes. This is when it gets quiet. But this is when it gets harder. Whatever you do, do not look.

I've trained for this. I'm prepared. I'm ready.

The thing is, the two minutes take forever to pass. I stare at my digital watch to keep track.

The breathing is louder than I've ever heard it before. It's all around me and this creature is so enormous, it's not all in the room with me. It seems like this is the small edge of something more massive than I can imagine. Maybe more massive than anyone knows. The breathing vibrates in the earth beneath my feet, shudders in the walls that slope up either side of me.

And whatever you do, do not speak to it. It will say anything to get you on its side.

"Let me go." The voice doesn't match the breathing. It's a small voice, like from a person. A very sad, exhausted sort of person.

I'm not supposed to listen. I swipe the flashlight and stab and stare at the blackness beneath me.

"I can't do this anymore, please let me go." Not only is the voice small, it's young. Young like a teenager?

Do not look.

"Shea? Is that you?" It says.

They never said it would know my name.

"You're the youngest. Aren't you? Like Mama and Dad didn't go have a sixth kid, did they?"

I know I'm not supposed to, but I look. My flashlight shines on the back wall of the basement and on the undulating fleshy whiteness that drapes out into the darkness behind it, there are chunky black glasses stuck into the wall. The glasses are fused to a face of human flesh, colored in the peachy tawniness of our family. Flat blue, tired eyes gaze out at me.

It's Toby.

The noise that comes out of me takes the shape of an "oh," but is half moan and all cry.

It's Toby, but not. His face is still colored like ours, but the white flesh starts around the rim of his hairline and goes back into the shadowed pale walls and the creature. The red glow is a pulsating light in the rippling pallid flesh far enough below his face it's where his heart would be. The red glow sits in a human length lump of reptilian flesh where the rest of his body should be. But it's not human shaped, that lump. Not really.

My moan lets loose the tears and I say, "I don't understand."

"It'll be your firstborn, too, you know." When he turns his head, the flesh around it quivers outward. He isn't trapped in it, so much as part of it.

I think of Mama and how we aren't allowed to mention Toby. The tears come in gulps now. "I don't..."

"The firstborn of the lastborn. I feed the house. I feed the happiness. I hold back..." his eyes flash a deeper glowing red and the voice that groaned awake echoes through the being, "...this thing."

"How could she let you?" *Did she give him to it? Does she know? Of course she knows. This is why she won't let us talk about Toby. Jesus. How does she send her kids down into this every year?*

He smiles dully. "It's just how things are done."

"What happens if you aren't here to hold it back?"

"It won't work for us. It'll get out of control. It's most powerful on Solstice, feeding off the dark and the cold. That's why I need help today."

"What is it?"

He doesn't answer. He breathes deep and the walls around him shudder with it. "You'll be asked to say an oath when you go back upstairs. They'll let you rest first and then tomorrow, you'll say the oath. You'll be asked to become part of this."

"But we've always lived here. We've always fought this." *This means that Martina knows? Jeffrey knows? Is this why Carl won't come home anymore?*

"You're the youngest. Mama was the youngest. It'll be your firstborn." Maybe this is why Mama is so hard this year. So…closed off. She knows I'm the youngest. Which means what again? It means I get the house but is this the price?

Toby says, "Honestly, I can't wait to be released."

"I don't. Released?"

"Your two minutes…"

I look at my watch. He's right. But now. I can't.

He insists, "They'll expect it."

Swipe, Swipe, stab. The poker barely touches his trunk, but he lets loose a roar of anger and indignation that make me stab an extra time, hitting flesh.

"That's right. That's the way to do it." He sounds tired. So tired.

"Did you talk to Carl? To Jeffrey? To Martina?"

"Carl is the only one who listened."

"Carl is the only one who left."

The house sighs. Toby sighs. It's one; it's double, but the sigh is large and vibrates the house around me. "I don't blame him really. He was older. What's there to lose? He couldn't live with it. And he had a choice," he added. Was that bitterness? He sighed again and I thought of all the times the house had sighed. Was it really Toby sighing? He said, "Carl really loved you, you know."

This hits me in the chest and the lump wells up in my throat again. So much of every part of my life is tangled up in this and I can't make sense of the new patterns. Each thread thrums through years of information. Carl left, but Carl loved me. Mama knows about me as youngest. Mama gave up her firstborn kid. Dad has known about this all along. Martina and Jeffrey know and are okay with it. They are okay with it and Carl was not. Carl left. Carl loved me.

I say, "I miss him."

His laugh strangles in a growl and he says, "I do too. He was the only one who really talked to me. Until now."

Tears come to my throat and my voice chokes. "Mama let this happen to you."

The flesh around him is rumbling, rippling, pushing forward.

Toby says, "Two minutes."

I can barely lift the poker, but I swipe and stab. It roars, he roars, but the rumbling recedes.

I said, "I don't understand why."

"It feeds this."

"But what *is* it?"

All of the noise stops for a moment as if the entire being is contemplating the question. The house breathes really really deep and Toby says. "It's something our ancestors brought over. I know that. On the boats. Waaay back."

"But why our family?"

"I don't know. And I don't know if we're the only ones. I do know our country wouldn't be what it is without it. It's a hunger. A need. A power. It got us here alive. It killed off the Indians. It grew with land theft. It grew with slavery, it grew into manifest destiny. It grew with railroads and money and stocks and greed. It grew with erasure. It made our people…what they are." He says the last line bitterly.

Our people. I don't know what that means. "But that's not. That's not *us.* That's, like ancestor crap." I know about smallpox. I know about slavery. But this is 1978. We're free to be you and me, we had the Bicentennial, our country is freedom, liberty for all, Sesame Street, women's lib.

"We live here. This is our ancestors. This is us. Two minutes."

It takes me a moment to process, but the rumble starts again, and I swipe, stab, Toby roars and we are quiet.

After a minute, I say, "The deed. We've owned this place forever."

Toby's laugh, one "ha" is reiterated in the gut of the beast, resonating. "Own. That's your problem right there."

I will have a kid one day, and that kid will have to do this. For. The house? I inherit the house because I'm the youngest. Mama knows this. When did she tell Dad this? Did he know when they were married? Did he know when they first had Toby?

"Why? How do we make it stop?"

And Toby starts talking long and low with two minute intervals of action/ reaction as we fight the beast and work it through.

We go on like this until morning. Talking in the two minutes between. Trying to figure a way out of it. It might be as simple as the freeze that's coming in two days. It will definitely ruin Christmas, but it's the only way out. And I can't do this. I can't be part of this. And I can't run like Carl, knowing Toby is down here. Stuck. Knowing that the whole family is still doing this. Every year. And knowing what it started, all of this. And what might it bring?

I don't even know if I want kids, but I can't have this at the other end of that decision.

I can't.

The dawn comes. I tell Toby I love him. I mean it in a fierce, protective way I only felt about Carl and Martina before I knew she knew. Yesterday. That thought makes me so tired.

Toby goes to sleep. His eyes close, the red glow inside the pale flesh fades and the fleshiness takes him in, first creeping up and covering his face and his glasses, then folding over him and receding back into the shadows in the basement. I sit down and just start blubbering. I imagine, aside from that first meltdown when he first told me, I was being strong for him all those hours. And we have a plan now, but I have to go back up to face that family who knows about this, to that family that was okay with this. I loved them so much, but it's like that love has been replaced with a giant black hole of anger and disappointment. It's too much.

I try to slow my breathing and get the blubbering under control. Did Martina cry? I do this trick Mama taught me to stop the crying: you recite "The Owl and the Pussycat" in your head until your breathing comes under control.

All these years. I forgot to ask him how time moves for him. Is it the same as us? Does he spend minute after minute in the darkness until the next Solstice?

Not this time.

I get to my feet and make my way up the stairs as slowly as I'd come down them, my knees weary, my poker and flashlight impossibly heavy. The poker smacks each step as I can't even raise that arm anymore. *Step, clunk, step, clunk.* I raise my flashlight hand enough to knock on the door once and I hear Dad lift the bar from the other side. I gulp back my tears. I'm not ready to talk to anyone about this yet. I'm not prepared to create even the false story that I'm part of this. I mostly want bed. Did Carl cry, too?

They are all standing on the other side of the door looking at me anxiously.

Well, most of them. Mama isn't there. For the first Solstice ever, she stayed in bed. I wonder if it's because she knows. The last born's first born... She knows, remembers herself at that age. She knows what it means.

Martina says, "How was it?"

Dad says with some ridiculous relief in his voice, "Well, now everyone knows, no more secrets."

Jeffrey says, "You okay?"

They don't look the same to me. I hate their faces. All of them.

I say, "But why?" This stops them. And I cough. *Has no one asked this question before?*

Dad says, "It's. It's a hard truth, honey. It's just the way things work around here.

"But why can't we stop it?"

Martina makes an *oooh* noise like I'm in trouble.

Dad sighs. "Go to bed honey. It'll make more sense after you've slept some. It's a lot to take in. Especially for you."

I eat a piece of cold apple pie they've left out for me and drink a big glass of milk and then I head up the stairs to bed. *When did this house get so many stairs? This house.* An ache and weakness shakes each leg as I pull it up another step. Everything is heavy now.

I sleep until noon the following day. I wake up with a sour mouth, a splitting headache, and a determination to end this nonsense. Martina is gone. I reach over and grab the aspirin and water waiting for me on my bedside table. The solution is simple, really. And if no one else is going to help Toby, I will.

When I go downstairs, Dad's in his study working the jigsaw puzzle he started at Thanksgiving. It's some ridiculously hard to decipher jungle scene, but I think on his non-drinking days it's how Dad makes it to Solstice. He's almost done, which is just as well because present wrapping will take over this area shortly. He's whistling, that heavy cloud of Solstice lifted. It was always a relief to see this in him, but now it feels sinister.

I don't want to even have to deal with him, but I'm expected to check in and have a talk. I can't remember ever wanting to completely avoid Dad, aside from maybe after our weird sex talk two years before. But this isn't that kind of avoidance. I can't stand the idea of him. All of the conversations we've had around Solstice are rushing back through my head for their hidden meaning. And what felt like his caring, his supporting me, his "attagirl," is really something so terrible I can't sort it yet.

He's bent over the puzzle so far I can see his little round bald patch, and when I see his hunched shoulders, his hand paused with a puzzle piece hovering over the table, I want to start yelling, raging at him. I want to go back to yesterday when I believed he only wanted the best for his children. Back to the him I really loved. I want to burst out crying. Instead, I clear my throat.

"Hey kiddo!" He's cheerful. *What the hell?*

I say, "So I gotta do an oath or something?"

He stands up rubbing his palms on his legs as he does so. He says, "Yes, yes, let me see." And he goes around to behind Grandpa Massey's desk, opening the drawer with his key. I never even thought Mama and Dad locked things up. I wonder what Grandpa locked up in there.

Grandpa, who knew when he sent Mama down. The awfulness of all of this layers back through everything I loved about this place.

My birthright.

This house may only go back to 1902, but Mama's family has lived on this property in one form or another since they moved here in 1603. I start to think the basement predates the house. I start thinking of oldests and youngests in mobcaps, in britches, with muskets. I wonder if The Wangunk lived here before and if the basement was like that then. But Toby said our family brought this here. This horror. Is it the sort of thing you dig a hole for and plant? Is this a space where something bad happened and it's haunted?

This land belonged to the Wangunk tribe before. Not like "belonging" was something they really thought about land. But whatever my ancestors brought started here. And grew.

Dad pulls out a piece of paper that's yellow and thick like a page from one of our super old Oz books. He hands it to me. I take it carefully. It's in weird old timey English and Dad says, "the Fs are Ss." I tremble it out pronouncing as best I can. It has so many therebys and heretofores and flowery language I can barely parse it, so maybe that makes it easier. Something about holding back evil. *Yeah with Toby*. Something about recompensing for something and claiming and protecting the land and of course, something about silence until death.

I cross my fingers the whole time.

Protect the land. It's not our land, is it? If you really think about it. And the house will go to me. So we can keep this shit going on for more generations.

When I finish it an, "Amen," comes out before I think to stop it and Dad chuckles. I keep my eyes to the ground because if I look up he'll read what utter bullshit I found that. I say, "Uh. Thanks. Okay."

Dad lays his hand on my shoulder which only reminds me how sore my muscles are from the battle. He says, "I'm proud of you honey. I'm glad we can share all of *this* with you now," his arms go wide motioning around the great wild room, the slave ship on the mantelpiece—why didn't I ever think that was weird before? I knew it was a slave ship. The ancient desk, the deed, the old books, the house itself. Dad's domain. Our domain. Our inheritance.

His hands float back to my shoulders. "Now, do you have any questions?"

I gauge my response. What does Dad expect the prior me to do? To say? But I can't. I don't have the energy to fake anything. I look up only then and say, "Dad, can I just take a day or two? I'm worn out."

I wait as he decides whatever and his face goes from eager to dead and his tone joins it. "Of course you can."

I can't help but feel I've disappointed him somehow and my first impulse is to say something to make the light come back in his eyes. He was so enthused just a moment ago. What does he need from me now? Were any of the others overjoyed about that awfulness in the basement?

Like all of the other lies in my life, I count on my Dad's unconditional love for me. I count on how much he validates me as a person, how he sees me and supports me, be it with homework or art supplies or books I'd like to read. I count on the quiet company we keep, the trips to the hardware store, the grocery, the Pizza Palace, the way he called me peanut when I was very small and then kiddo later with the same amount of love. But now it all feels like he was grooming me so he could hold on to this giant desk and this den, his ship's model, and his jigsaw puzzles. He loves this more than he loves me. He loves this more than he loves his firstborn son. Did he marry Mama knowing all this or did she break him in slowly?

Only a year ago, Dad said, "I married this house," in a pleased way that made me feel cozy and comfortable but that now echoes back with a chilling meaning.

But Toby and I have a plan. And I can't do anything about it for two days, anyway. Right now is my last day with full television privileges, so I do as expected, grab the remote from Jeffrey and stare at *Bewitched* while I try to sort things out. As long as I stay glued to the tube, maybe no one will try to talk to me.

The weather forecast foretold a cold snap, but when it hits, the temperatures plunge below what anyone expected. What was meant to bottom out around eleven degrees is going to get to negative two. A twenty-year record.

I walk around the house one last time that night, lingering in the kitchen, remembering summers before, when I didn't know. I take in bright yellow walls of the kitchen and the wood of the table, Gainsly's snuffle as he roots for incidental crumbs or bits of something from dinner. I feel a gaping sadness, not for the fact that this won't be here anymore, but for the fact that it's already lost to me. None of it means what I thought it did. I wander in through the dining room. The big top is still on the table from Thanksgiving so we can have Christmas there. We put the small round top back on the table after the holidays have gone. Two china closets stand sentry on the opposite door from the dining room. One was inherited from Dad's mom, one has always been here, and both are laden with generations of china, from Wedgewood to Royal Minten. Federalist silver, real Revereware. I used to stare at these treasures thinking of their history, their meaning to the family as each new generation married and treasures were passed down, added on. Now they loom, heavy with generations of knowing. The family pictures hang scattered on the wall of the front hall, all without Toby. Goofy pictures of me and Jeffrey in the back yard, sweaty from the summer, of Martina and me in matching dresses. What did Toby do those summers? Did he know they were passing?

I'm getting maudlin. No one will be hurt. It's just a stupid house with a bad secret. And then it will be over. I'm not sure how I'll deal with my folks after but who knows, maybe breaking out of this awful Solstice cycle will free Mama. No more black moods.

It will free Toby, and that's what matters.

I kiss Mama goodnight that night for the first time since Solstice. This time I mean it. It's an *I'll take care of you* promise kiss. It's an ending the cycle kiss. It's a kiss for everything she's carried. I try not to think about what it means to give up one's firstborn. She goes *mmmmm* and throws her arm around me squeezing. She then turns back to her knitting. A scarf for someone for Christmas. Mama's always knitting and we never know who it's for. The surprise will be who opens the package with the cornflower blue scarf inside. But not this year, I guess.

I kiss Dad in a cursory way because I'm not really talking to him yet. Mama doesn't have much of a choice, but he joined this lie. Out of love for her? When did he know he'd have to give up Toby? Before they were married or after he had him? Or has he always been that way? I wonder how Mama and Dad treated Toby, were they assholes to him so he'd be an asshole and it would be easier? Or did they give him a ton of love because they knew what he'd have to carry?

I poke my head in Jeffrey's room where he's tooling with his guitar. He looks up and noses a greeting. I say, "Good night," and turn to go.

It's just me and Toby now.

We wait until everyone is asleep. We creep up the stairs into the attic in what used to be Toby's bedroom. Toby before. Toby the boy. It's now filled with boxes of things, cast off chairs, a walker from when Gram had her hip replaced. Gram knew too, what Solstice meant. She sacrificed a child. She knew her oldest grandson would be sacrificed. Gram of the homemade cinnamon buns and backyard golfing tee. Gram of the late-night fairy tales.

We fight our way through the stuff to the radiator. We turn the knob until it turns off and make our way back through the ocean of cardboard to the other side of the room and the bathroom. We go to the sink that stands next to that clawfoot tub where we took long soaks after Mama told us the truth, what we had to do. After she told us what we needed to sacrifice for the sake of the family. Before we went into the cold forever. Mama held our shoulder that time, led us down the stairs, into the back and even when we said, *no, no you can't make me*, she did, and she handed us over as the flesh surrounded us. The squelching sound as the monster released her oldest sister, our aunt, the roaring sound as it stretched to pull us in, It was so loud we didn't even hear if she cried for us. Did she cry? Did she ever even love us?

And we are fixing this now. No one should have to do this again. We'll both be free. We are unwinterizing in winter. The cold snap is coming tonight, and it will do the work for us. We turn on the water pipe to the attic bathroom. The water will flow into that pipe, it will be too cold up here from the snap and if we work from the basement and the attic, it will go more quickly.

Here in the basement, we know our powers. We know our powers to hold back, but also to let go a little. It hates the furnace; the furnace is warmth and light. It can't wait to get to it. We let go a little and it swells and grows, filling the basement, thrilled to be given its limbs. Nothing to fight back here, our wills are united as we stretch and stretch until the flesh reaches the furnace. This is what the parents didn't tell us for the fighting: we mustn't let it reach the furnace. We followed orders, not knowing what we were fighting back. But without me to hold it in place, we grow up around the furnace and it is hot, and we don't like it, but we don't care, for soon we will all be free.

What's a little pain in the face of a lifetime? We are weak after Solstice, they never explained to us that we'd work together, the siblings. That was our sacrifice. Working to fight back the cold, then only one of us gets to go upstairs to life again.

No one else will have to do this again, that's for sure.

The pain is certainly no more than being fought back, but there is sizzling, a bit of smoke. In five seconds without oxygen, the fire is snuffed and the burning stops. Time and cold will do their work now. We will soon be free.

We bleed the radiator in the attic room so it also floods with water. Who knows the pipe that will burst first?

We go to bed as instructed and wait. Somewhere in the middle of the night, when we have just dozed off, there is a distant clank from the attic bathroom and the water begins to flow. We grab our bag of stuff and move downstairs. We listen outside our door to the hallway where the family sleeps, but there is no noise at all aside from Mama's snore that matches the breathing of the house. You would have to work hard to hear that water.

Soon. Soon we will be released from this. All of us will be released.

Then there is a clank from the bathroom on the second floor.

Unlike with fire, no one will be hurt. All of us can get out in time. And this will finally be over.

I wait in the front hall at the bottom of the stairs until a trickle creeps into a cold wet patch on my leg and I stand. The stairwell is becoming a waterfall, slowly, like when you first turn the hose on the Slip 'n Slide. Four more clanks and the trickle turns into a rush, and an actual waterfall is in place when a door bursts open upstairs and I hear Dad, "What the fuck is going on here?" Dad's not a swearer.

As if he'd willed it, that is the moment the water, pooling on the floor of the upstairs hallway starts sheeting down off the edge of the floor where it meets the bannister, like on Pirates of the Caribbean, making Dad's consequent yells distant and warbly as it creates a barrier over the stairwell.

I take my bag and wait by the front door. I watch the water sheet over the stairwell, the mini waterfall on the last curve of the landing as the smells and presence of the house change from dry warmth, food and books, to wet wool, soaking antiques, metallic flow and water, water. The sheet of water is colored as the sun rises behind the stained-glass window. I loved that window. But we are saving Toby, so anything we're doing is worth it. We're saving any child I might have one day.

It's a full ten minutes before my family walks through that sheet of water, like they're coming from another dimension. My Dad first, wet, bedraggled, his eyes fall on me, waiting there and relief crosses his face. He hollers back through the barrier to another world, "I found her!" He's soaking wet. Jeffrey follows, then Mama, then finally with a grand noisy smatter because she had the brains to use an umbrella, Martina.

Dad says, "What are you waiting for, open the door!"

As I open it, there's an enormous creaking and crash upstairs, shaking the house followed by a house-wide moan that I worry is Toby. Something has fallen or shifted. We all look back, incredulous as the stream of water coming down the stairwell turns into a flood. There's a creaking and groaning underlying the mad sound of rushing water and Dad herds us outside into the sparkling cold. I had prepared, putting the spare blankets from the TV room on the curb. I hand them to Martina and Jeffrey who take them without question and Mama whose brow furrows and Dad who snatches it, throws it around his shoulders and runs next door. Likely to find a phone.

After a long minute, Mama says, "Shea…"

But then Dad comes running back toward us. "Half an hour."

Mama says, "Half an hour, look at it!"

Water is flooding out the front door, as it was meant to, but there is something shifting in the house. Is it off plumb, or has it always been that way because of the hill? It creaks and groans as something larger shifts and falls inside.

By the time the water company gets there to turn off the main, it has definitely started listing to the left down the hill. Water is pouring out from between the clapboards on the second floor. The man from the city is older with an orange stocking cap pulled down over his ears under his white helmet. He jumps back in his truck and fetches a long metal tong-like thing. He looks up at the house disbelieving and my Dad coughs to shake him out of it. He clears his throat, pops the lid off a cover in the ground and twists the main shut.

We all look back at the house. I wonder if Toby drowned. I wonder where we will move, how this will change everything. How pissed Mama will be when she learns the truth. Or will she maybe be relieved? To be released from this cycle? I imagine us all living in an apartment in town. Life containable, conquerable. We can still do all our regular city stuff, Pizza Palace, trips to the shops on Main Street to see the decorations. But it will be just us. Without the house. The history. The weight. Dad's job can afford an apartment. I only have five more years before I get out of here anyway. Maybe I can look up Carl and he'll let me move in with him. I'll get a job. We'll be fine. And without all that time training in winter, who knows what we can do?

We watch, but it takes a few moments for the water to slow at all. Once it does, as if water were the only thing holding it together, the listing turns into real movement and the house goes completely crooked, sliding off of and into its foundation. The roof, once proud and arched, caves in on itself. Glass shatters, beams break, and it falls. It sighs as it does so. There is this sense of…release.

Toby is free.

I'm free.

My kid is free.

My family is free.

I smile.

Mama says, "Shea…"

I turn to her saying, "It's over, Mama. All done. We don't have to do this anymore."

I can feel Jeffrey and Martina turning to face me, but I don't take my eyes off Mama.

Dad says, "Shea, honey." The endearment has turned to acid.

Mama says, "What did you do?" in such a poisonous voice I don't think I've ever heard before.

"I set Toby free. I set all of us…" but my confidence fades as her face moves from fury to sadness to fear.

"We were the guardians."

"Of the house, I know."

Mama collapses onto the lawn, her legs splayed funny, her fuzzy bunny jammy pants a stark pink against the dead grass. She sobs, "No, no, no, no, no, no."

"Mama?"

Dad starts in, "Jesus Christ, Shea, did you think about consulting with any of us before you made this enormous decision for the family?"

"Mama?"

She looks up at Dad and swallows. "We have to go. Now." She turns to me and says, "It's not Toby you freed honey. You freed it."

She looks back at the house. The water has slowed to a trickle running down the sidewalk. The bright yellow wood of the outside of the house is mixed with the dark wood of the inside, and both are mixed with something pale and terrifying. It's then that I see them, the reaching fronds, the branches of white flesh. Growing out from the house's front, reaching, stretching across the yard. Toward us? Toward everything.

SPRING

MARTINA

She didn't want the house? Fine. But she didn't have to fucking ruin everything just because she wussed out of her family duty.

Worked out in the end. I mean, Dad had to get Jeffrey down there tout suite. I told Dad they should really go and fetch Carl, but he said there wasn't time and Carl was a grown man now and might very well not come. Jeffrey blubbered and whimpered, and Shea tried to throw her skinny ass between them, but she slipped on the ice and went down. She was screaming and crying and her voice was so thin in the morning air. Mama just sat there next to the fire hydrant on the parkway, wrapped in a blanket and shaking her head while Dad stormed up the front stairs holding Jeffrey by the upper arm. Jeffrey skidded on the ice, but Dad held him upright with more strength than I knew he had.

Top of the porch was hard to figure with the house a pile of roofing and clapboard and wood and crap. Dad stood there, Jeffrey wailing, "No…" Everyone knows Jeffrey's a pussy.

The house knew what to do. Or the thing. Because this house was kaput, Shea made sure of that. It was so fast. Dad standing there, Jeffrey wailing and then these filthy white fleshy limbs, pinkish in the morning light, snatched Jeffrey by the ankles, wound up around his chest and pulled him down so fast it surprised his wail into stopping. There was a sucking noise and the ground trembled as it settled beneath us. The white roots that had formed in the yard pulled themselves back down and disappeared under the torn up grass and dirt.

They sent Shea to Choate. *Boarding* school. I'd be jealous and all, but this means I get the house. I know what you're thinking, I mean, you saw what happened. But this happens every once in a while. Some family member wants to be a hero. Wants to make it stop. Wants to share the wealth and comes up with some melting pot bullshit. Some equality for all line. We all know how this works, how it's been working since our ancestors first landed and took the land that was destined for them.

We nurture this thing that we brought here, that gave us all of this. And we enjoy the fruits of our labor, sea to shining sea.

The last person who pulled a Shea was great Uncle Joe who wrote bad poetry, burned down the house, and then went off to college. That was 1901.

But the fun part is now, when we rebuild, I tell them what what I want. Mama's excited for me. But with Jeffrey in the basement and Carl gone and Shea not trustworthy, it's gonna be me down there battling that thing every year. So I want one of those House & Garden ultra-modern specials, big glass windows, travertine floors you could roller skate on and a hooded fireplace in the center of a giant living room. I want a conversation pit.

Maybe we can have a pool.

Acknowledgements

A huge thank you to editor extraordinaire Jennifer Barnes, for all her work on this book, to John Edward Lawson to the larger conversations we have and providing this pathway. Thanks to the RDS team, especially Rhonda Jackson-Garcia and Erin Al-Mehairi, it felt like a homecoming.

Thanks to my beta readers on *Safer*, Nicole D. Sconiers, Yuvi Zalkow and Andromeda Romano-Lax. And a special thank you to Ana Chaidez, for the sensitivity read and to Seth Fischer for hiking the Hollywood Reservoir and Wolf's Lair on a very hot day so I could get the landscape right. Thanks for my previous Hollywood bosses who taught me so much by allowing me at the table in that world which was most…inspiring.

Thanks to Lisa Morton and Ellen Datlow, who inadvertently gave me the writing prompt for *Family Solstice*; their constant work in the field of horror is a daily inspiration to me. Thank you to Kate Jonez for putting so much into *Family Solstice* in its first iteration and for throwing the ultimate pandemic Second Life launch party.

To the Art, Tacos, Fiction (and Poetry!) San Clam gang for being amazing company, for their quiet creative energy and a gorgeous weekend and to Gen and Kendra Maruyama for providing that space.

To my parents who always stood up to and fought against the inequities they saw about them in the workplace or in life in general. At the time, they were radical for flying in the face of the system from which they benefitted, when everyone looked at them like they were crazy or accused them of being pains in the ass. To them it was common sense. Shea is for them. My apologies to them and those who love the place for nestling systemic evil in our basement, but 45 Lawn was too awesome not to write about and its destruction too gothic.

Thanks to my brothers for tormenting me with Pinkeltein, the long-lost made-up brother who made me feel there was always someone missing at Thanksgiving. He was the inspiration for Toby, and a bit for Carl.

Thanks to my constant companion, Ko, especially for seeing me through the path of destruction of my childhood home that inspired Solstice. My parents and that house would have taken me with them if it weren't for his unconditional care, common sense, and his ability to make me laugh.

Thanks to Reed, my one-woman hype man and Jack, my mellowest companion in these trying times. They both have taught me more than they know and have made me a better person.

About the Author

Kate Maruyama's novel *Harrowgate* was published by 47North and her novella *Halloween Beyond: The Gentleman's Suit* by Crystal Lake Publishing. *Family Solstice* in its original iteration was published by Omnium Gatherum Media and was named Best Fiction Book of 2021 by *Rue Morgue Magazine*. Her short work has appeared in *Asimov's*, *Analog,* and *Uncharted* among other journals and in numerous Anthologies including *Winter Horror Days, December Tales* and *Halloween Carnival Three*. She is a member of the SFWA and HWA where she serves on the Diverse Works Inclusion Committee and she sits on the board of Women Who Submit, an organization that works to create gender and racial parity in publishing.

CPSIA information can be obtained
at www.ICGtesting.com
Printed in the USA
JSHW020205120623
43058JS00001B/46